amor

the support.

Laramie

Meant to Be

Book #1 of the Heaven Hill Series

By Laramie Briscoe

Copyright

Edited by: Lindsay Gray Hopper

Cover Art by: Kari Ayasha of Cover to Cover Designs

Biker image Copyright: Ljupco Smokovski | Dreamstime.com

Model image Copyright: Kaponia Aliaksei

Dedication

To my husband who has always encouraged me to never give up on my dreams. I want to thank him for spending many hours listening to me talk about this and sacrificing time together so that I could make this happen.

To my grandmother who gave me my first romance novel and my mom who encouraged my love of reading.

To my dad who never got to see his dreams come true.

This is for all of you!

Summary

Single mother.

Laid off factory worker.

Drug runner for the Heaven Hill Motorcycle Club.

When Denise Cunningham is served with foreclosure papers on her birthday it's the last straw in a long line of bad luck. Sitting and crying about things has never been how she solved her problems, but this time she decides to do just that. A phone call interrupts her pity party and changes the course of her life forever.

Loyal brother.

Grease monkey mechanic.

Vice President of the Heaven Hill Motorcycle Club.

William Walker Jr., known as Liam to his club, needs a new recruit that is just naïve enough and desperate enough to do what he asks without question. When Denise Cunningham lands in his lap, he decides to hire her - not because he wants to, because he has to.

Neither are comfortable in their new roles, but he needs help and she can't stand to lose anything else.

As bullets fly and a local Bowling Green, KY reporter works to bring the club down, Liam and Denise find themselves getting closer to one another. When the stakes get high and outside forces try to keep them away from each other, they have to decide if they really are meant to be.

Prologue

Denise Cunningham pulled back the curtains covering the window pane in her front door with shaky hands. The knock that had sounded moments before wasn't the gentle knock of a friend over for a visit. Staring back at her through the glass, she saw two Warren County Sheriff's deputies holding papers. Dread rolled up in her throat as her stomach began to churn. She let the blinds fall and took two deep breaths before she unlocked the door and faced the men standing on the other side. As she stepped out, the brightness of the sun assaulted her eyes, the warmth of the summer day made it even more difficult to breathe past the lump in her throat.

"Denise Cunningham?" The taller of the two asked.

Not trusting her voice, she could only nod her head in acknowledgement of who she was.

With cold efficiency, he handed her the papers in his hands. "Denise Cunningham, I'm serving you with papers from Kentucky Housing." He produced a pen and request-ed her signature.

In minutes it was over. The scene she had dreaded most over the last few months had come to fruition. Unless she could come up with six months back mortgage, she would lose her home. She stood frozen in shock as the officers walked away from the door and headed back to their patrol car. It almost made her laugh – the fact that they felt she, a single mother, was dangerous enough to warrant two deputies. As they pulled away, she realized her neighbors watched. Shame and embarrassment caused her face to burn as she slammed her door shut.

Tears came now, along with shakes that wracked her body. "God, please help me," she whispered as she opened the packet of paperwork they had left with her. "What am I going to do?" Through the tears, she read the legal papers in her trembling hands. The amount due was more than she had seen in years. Especially now that her hours had recently been cut. She was officially screwed.

The shrill ringing of her cell phone broke into her freakout. A number she had never seen before displayed on the screen, and she wondered if she should answer it. Along with the money she owed on her home, she owed thousands to credit card companies. They had also begun to hound her. Should she take the chance and answer it or let the voicemail pick it up? As she debated, her finger hit the *accept* button of its own accord.

"Hello?"

"Denise, this is Roni," the voice on the other end greeted.

Roni was in fact Sharon Walker, another employee at the big box store where Denise had found a temporary job. They'd only spoken a time or two, and Denise hadn't actually been sure the other woman would ever call her. To say this was a surprise was an understatement. But at this point, anything that took her mind off of what had just happened was welcome.

"Hey, Roni."

"Did I catch you at a bad time? It took you a while to answer. I'm gonna ask you for a favor, so if you can't do it, just let me know," she forged ahead in a rush.

A bad time? Was it couth to tell a mere acquaintance that your home was about to be foreclosed on?

Clearing her throat Denise said, "Not at all. What can I help you with?" Accepting a favor for someone would possibly get her out of the house, the house that soon would no longer be hers. The walls were closing in, and she needed something to do. She needed something to work out halfway good for once instead of all the gloom and doom.

"Can you cover my shift for me tonight? I've got a little bit of an emergency with my brother, and I'm gonna need a few hours."

Denise bit her lip. She had heard rumblings about Roni's brother. Word around town had it that he was part of a major outlaw biker gang called the Heaven Hill Motorcycle Club. Whatever Roni would be doing to help her brother would probably be illegal. Would that make Denise an accomplice?

"Would it make you a what?" Roni asked as Denise stood frozen with the phone to her ear.

Shit. She'd said that out loud. "Nevermind. I'll cover for you. What time do I have to be there?" Anything would be better than sitting here, worrying about things she had no control over.

Roni rattled off a time that would only allow her minutes to get dressed, head out the door, and make it there just in time to clock in. Quickly they hung up. Depression threatening to take over, Denise shoved the packet of paperwork under the pillow of her couch. With any luck neither of her children would see it. Their lives had been in as much upheaval as hers. They didn't need to see this too – she felt like a failure as their mother.

Pulling out of her Plum Springs subdivision, Denise made her way to Louisville road which took her to the interstate. The interstate would take her less time than going through town. She made sure to take in her surroundings. Unless a miracle happened or she hit the lottery, her days living in this neighborhood were numbered. A red light stopped her right before she hit the interstate. To the left, blue lights could be seen swirling on top of police cars. Men were being handcuffed and put in back seats two at a time. It wasn't unusual to see arrests right next to the interstate, but this time she noticed an influx of motorcycles. The gas station on Duntov Way, situated between a fast food restaurant and a liquor store, usually didn't see a lot of motorcycles. The exception being Harley Weekend at the local dragstrip. With keen eyes, she got a good look at the patches that adorned the backs of the leather vests, or cuts as they called them, the men wore.

"Fuck," she breathed, recognizing the patch on most of the men. The Heaven Hill insignia inside a skull. The bottom rocker on the cut indicated this was the Bowling Green Chapter.

It was the Heaven Hill Motorcycle Club, and, if she wasn't mistaken, she had just seen Roni's brother get put in the back of a sheriff's patrol car. Probably by the same officers that had just served her. If there was one thing she knew, it was that all hell was about to break loose in small-town Kentucky.

Chapter One

R oni Walker sighed deeply as she stood outside the city jail. Unfortunately, in the past few months the employees had come to know her by name. Every time she turned around, someone in the MC was getting into trouble. Being a female, she wasn't privy to club information, so most of the time she flew in the dark and under the radar. This, however, was beginning to piss her off. Grabbing a peppermint from her pocket, she waited for the two members of the MC she'd been dispatched to bail out. This place gave her the heebie jeebies and she bit down hard on the candy, cursing as a sharp edge sliced her cheek.

Trying to keep her mind off of what could possibly be going down inside the jail, she took in her surroundings. The beautiful South Central Kentucky day belied the butterflies in her stomach. The warmth of the sun beat down on her head, and the sky was a deep blue and cloudless. If she had been someone else, part of another family, she might be out on a picnic. She might be parked in a field with a boyfriend, enjoying some quiet time. Any of those scenarios would be better than what was happening at this moment. Instead, she paced back and forth, waiting for something to happen.

The entrance opened, and she looked up expectantly, smiling as she saw her brother and his best friend Tyler Blackfoot walked out.

"Thanks for coming to get us," Liam grinned.

She walked into the arms of her younger brother and squeezed him tight. It hurt her that he seemed to spend so much time going in and coming out of this building. "I wouldn't let you stay in there, Liam."

"Tyler and I were fine, just like we always are. Did the guys get our bikes before they could be impounded?" he asked, looking up and down the street to see how she had arrived.

"They did," she nodded. "Everybody is at the club-house waitin' on us to get there, but we gotta be movin'. Some guys heard on the scanner that the local news media has picked up on this. You know what that means." She rolled her eyes in disgust.

Both men groaned. That meant hometown reporter, Meredith Rager, would be trying to get the scoop. Young and hungry, reckless and sometimes stupid. They'd had run-ins with her before, and after this long day she was someone they all wanted to avoid.

As they made their way up the street to Roni's car, they saw a news van pulling up next to the jail. Keeping their heads down, they walked swiftly and with purpose, hoping to deter the reporter. They had just made it into the car and shut the door when she caught up to them and knocked on the window. All three sent her a pointed glare as they drove off.

Hours later, Denise sat in the break room at her job watching the local news. She had called her thirteen-year-old twins and explained to them she'd had to pick up an extra shift. Neither of them had complained when they realized there was nothing more than a pound of hamburger in the fridge and some noodles in the pantry. When they told her to be careful on her drive home, tears had flooded her eyes and she realized that she didn't deserve them. They didn't deserve this lifestyle. When she first found out she was pregnant, the picture of what her life would be like had been so clear to her. She had known she would have to work hard, but she had also known for her offspring she would do it and like it. Denise knew that there would be tough times, but she never thought they would be *this* tough. What she had envisioned was struggling but making it through. For the first time ever, she now thought about giving up. It was a scary thought, but life had given her a hand she wasn't sure she could beat.

"Happy birthday," one of her co-workers yelled as he saw her. Glancing up at the news, she saw the date in the right-hand corner. It was August 1st. Was it sad she hadn't even remembered? What an amazingly shitty way to spend her birthday. Being served with foreclosure paperwork and getting called into her job. *Happy fucking birthday to me,* she thought.

Even more down than before, she turned her attention back to the news, which she watched mindlessly. She had no money, and God knew she was hungry. Hopefully watching the local anchors talk would help her keep her mind off the gnawing in her gut. Bottles of water were provided free of charge, and she'd already downed three of those. They hadn't helped, only made her have to go to the restroom a couple dozen times.

"In breaking news, members of the Heaven Hill Motorcycle Club were apprehended today as they were attempting to exit onto I-65 South. Sheriff's deputies found that William Walker Jr. and Tyler Blackfoot were wanted on outstanding warrants and in possession of narcotics with intent to distribute. Both were lodged in the county detention center where they were released on bond. A court date has not yet been set."

Denise grimaced. Roni would more than likely be upset about this turn of events. In the short time they had worked together, it was obvious that there was a lot of love for the outlaws she called family. Love, however, couldn't seem to hide illegal activities. Checking her watch, she realized her break was over.

It took everything that she had to get out of her seat and go clock back in. Life had dealt her some heavy blows today. Ones she would have to overcome, but that didn't mean she didn't want to lick her wounds for a little while. It seemed her whole life had been spent dealing with blows and licking wounds. That was neither here nor there at this point. Life went on no matter how the participants of said life handled it.

Four hours later, she clocked out for the night. Time had flown and dragged by at the same time. Her stomach growled loudly. Maybe she could find enough change in her car to buy a frozen pizza. It *was* her birthday after all. She was pretty sure the menial amount of food at home was now gone. Payday came in two days, and she wasn't sure how they would survive.

Walking out to her car, she realized that one thing had gone right. She had parked under a light. That would make it easier to look for and count her change. Her thoughts were so deeply consumed with praying that she had enough money for that frozen pizza, she didn't even notice the rest of her surroundings. As she unlocked her car door, a hand clamped down on her shoulder. Stifling a scream, she whirled around.

"Relax, I'm Roni's brother."

The man stood back from her with his hands up, away from his body. Her heart thundered, and she breathed heavily as she tried to calm down her racing heart.

"I didn't mean to scare you, but I yelled your name a few times and you didn't hear me."

She put her hand to her chest and focused on him, trying to slow down the beating of her heart. It was so loud, she was afraid he might hear it.

Pictures and far away glances did not do Liam Walker justice, she decided. Straight black hair hung almost to his shoulders, framing a face that held a few days growth of beard, blue eyes stood out brightly against the dark backdrop of his tanned face. Glancing down his body, she was almost disappointed that his arms were covered with a long sleeve shirt. She knew from conversations with Roni that he had one complete sleeve of tattoos on his left arm and the beginning of another on his right. His cut fit over his shirt and she could see his patches. Not sure what any of them meant, she pulled her purse closer to her body in a protective gesture, not that she had any money in it. The gesture wasn't missed by him. The eyes that had held compassion earlier now hardened. Obviously he took offense to the reaction deeply engrained in her psyche.

"Look lady, I'm not about to mug you out here in the open at the busiest piece of shit store this town has to offer. You're relatively safe. The only thing I'm here to do is offer you a thank you from my sister and the club. We appreciate you coverin' her shift so she could come get us out."

He held out two twenty dollar bills towards her.

Normally pride would keep her from readily accepting his money, but survival and the gnawing hunger in her gut strongly out-weighed pride and common sense.

Swallowing hard, she grabbed the money and shoved it into her pocket. Shame made her look around to see if anyone had witnessed her accepting his charity. Finally she found her voice. "I was happy to do it for Roni."

It didn't escape his attention, the words that went unspoken. That she didn't do it for him or his club.

"Either way, it's appreciated. Just wanted to let you know that. Roni would be here herself, but since she called in, she didn't want anyone to get suspicious."

The two of them stood in awkward silence. Both afraid to move, but each had very different reasons.

"Well thank you," she whispered, gesturing towards the money that now rested heavily in her pocket. "But please, don't bother me again. She's a co-worker and I was happy to help, but this isn't me."

"Same to you, maybe I'll see you around sometime," he said, grabbing his helmet and hopping on his bike.

As he roared out of the parking lot, she wondered if this would indeed be the last time she saw him. Something told her probably not. When she could no longer see the tail light of his bike, she turned around and went back inside to buy what groceries she could now afford.

Chapter Two

"We should use her."

Liam ground his back teeth together. He didn't agree with this at all. In fact, he thought the idea was about the stupidest thing he had ever heard. "Denise did what she did for Roni, not because she wanted to get an 'in' with the club. She made that very clear to me when I tried to say thank you for her part in getting us out. We don't need to use somebody who doesn't want to be involved. That's dangerous."

"I say we take a look at her financials. We might be able to persuade her," William Walker Sr. disagreed with his son. "Steele," he yelled. "I need you in here. Get me a credit report and everything else you can on Roni's friend, Denise Cunningham." He steepled his fingers together and rested his chin against them.

Dread settled over Liam at those words. There was a reason she had so readily picked up an extra shift at work on what he had been told was her birthday. When he'd approached her, he could see weariness in her eyes. It wasn't weariness caused by working too much, it was real tiredness. The kind that one got from being depressed and living paycheck to paycheck for too long. He'd seen it in some of the women who liked to hang around the clubhouse. They were women who were used specifically for sex, they weren't 'old lady' material. He didn't want this for her, didn't want any part of it.

With startling clarity, he knew that their bookkeeper and club secretary, Travis Steele, could find anything out about anyone. He was one of the best hackers in the world, and with the click of a mouse he could destroy a person's life.

"Let's see," Steele clicked a few buttons and chomped down on a piece of gum. "Denise Cunningham is the single mother of thirteen-year-old twins. One boy, one girl. She was just served a foreclosure notice on her home. Looks like she used to work at a local factory and lost her job when the economy tanked. There are lots of credit card bills, and it looks like collection companies are beating down her door."

Liam cursed. This was the exact kind of situation he didn't want the club to be in. He didn't want to have to use women to do a man's job. His father liked desperate. Liam thought desperate equaled mistakes.

"Get Roni to get her in here. Let's make her an offer she can't refuse," William told the group as he got up from the head of the table. The smarmy smile on his face made Liam rage.

"Wait a second old man, ain't we gonna take a vote on this?"

The group gasped at Liam's use of the phrase 'old man'. There were many things his father was. Asshole, vindictive, arrogant. But old man? That was going to earn him a lashing when this was over.

"Do we really need to? She'll work for us, and maybe we'll get free pussy too," he laughed flippantly.

Liam wasn't laughing. His gaze had instead turned very dark.

William recognized the look on his son's face. It was a look he'd seen in the mirror one or two times before. This was the kind of emotion he'd been looking to get out of his son for years. It was the kind of emotion Liam would need in order to run the club one day.

"That piss you off, son?" he goaded.

Liam carefully reeled his emotions back in. "Nah, I just wonder why we want a woman to do what our grunts can do. How are they gonna prove themselves if we never give them a chance? Jagger wants to be patched, and he never will if we don't give him somethin' to do. That's why we have Prospects."

William's eyes narrowed as he glared at the son who was daring to question his authority. "I'm president of this club. Until you get this patch," he pointed at the president's patch on his cut. "What I say goes, boy. I say we use her. Fuck no, this isn't going up for a vote. We need her, she probably needs us. End of discussion. You got anything else to say to me?"

He did have something to say, actually a lot to say, but knew this wasn't the time to bring it up. He'd bide his time and approach the old man when he wasn't so worried about how he would look to the rest of the club. He spit on the concrete floor to give him time to compose himself before facing his dad. "No, everything's fan-fucking-tastic."

"Glad I have your support VP," William bit off sarcastically. It was really a "fuck you" more than anything. "Ya know what? Why don't *you* go get her and bring her here? We'll be waiting."

Pissed, Liam grabbed his stuff and got up. He stood so suddenly the chair kicked back, shattering as it fell against the hard ground. Not bothering to pick it up, he stepped over it and stormed out of the clubhouse. Once he got to his bike, he hopped on and put the key in the ignition. At that point, he slowed down. Like always when he was about to go for a ride, his worries began to fade away. His heartbeat slowed and he could breathe normally. Chuckling to himself, he ran a hand through his hair before grabbing his helmet. If there was one person on this earth that could piss him off and turn him upside down, it was his father. He had been stupid and showed his true feelings – that he really didn't want to use someone who was not affiliated with the club – and old William had jumped on this show of weakness. When would he ever learn not to walk around with his heart on his sleeve?

"Try not to hurt her, okay?"

He glanced around at the small voice that spoke behind his back. It was Roni. "I don't even want to use her, but you know what William says goes."

"I hate that I got her involved in this," she worried, her hands twisting in front of her.

"It wasn't you, it's him. He's an asshole. He's ruthless. That's why he is who he is."

"Are you going to take someone with you?"

He grimaced. "No, I'm not showing up at a single mother's house with another large man. She'd probably think we're there to rape her."

"Can I give her a heads up?" Roni asked, a desperate plea showing in her eyes.

"Please do."

With those words he was gone, and Roni frantically dialed her friend.

Damnit, she had known it was a bad idea to accept money from Roni's brother. Denise hung up the phone and frantically looked around the house for her car keys. Was there any way she could leave before he showed up? Who was she kidding? He would probably be waiting for her when she came home. The kids were at a friend's house and would be staying the night. At least she didn't have to worry about them. A gentle knock sounded long before she was ready.

"Denise? It's Liam Walker. I need you to come answer the door."

She thought about telling him no or acting like she wasn't at home. She hadn't even heard his motorcycle pull up. She'd had no time to prepare.

"C'mon, don't make me come in there."

Would he really do that? Roni had told her he was the least of any of the evils that could have come to get her. A hard edge had laced his voice this time, telling her he would do whatever he had to do. His patience was obviously wearing thin. She walked over, took a deep breath, and opened the door.

"Come in." She hated the fear in her voice and how small it sounded, even to her ears.

He shut the door behind him, checking to make sure no one was watching. "Care if I have a seat?"

Liam Walker was larger than life to her. He may as well have been over seven feet tall and four hundred pounds. Her heart beat rapidly in her chest as she nodded. Purposely, she sat as far away from him as she could and still be in the same room.

"This ain't gonna work if you're scared of me. I'm not here to hurt you," he said softly, watching as she swallowed roughly.

"What exactly *are* you here to do?"

"The club needs a favor," he explained.

Denise didn't say anything. The leather of his cut creaked as he ran his hands along his jean-clad thighs. For some reason she was amazed at how big his feet looked in the large motorcycle boots he wore. She focused on that, trying not to acknowledge the fact that he had just asked her for a favor.

"What kind of favor?"

"It's dangerous, I'm not gonna lie to you. To be honest, I really didn't even want to bring you into this, but the old man wanted you here. We need some help transporting some drugs. You do it, you're paid well. You don't do it, we'll pretend like this never happened." It meant going against his dad, but he would do it to keep her safe.

She didn't believe him. How were they going to pretend like this never happened? There was no way they would allow her to say no and she knew it, but still she asked. "Can I have some time to think on it?"

He almost gave it to her but knew that if she thought about it too much she might turn him in or run. "No you can't think about it. You need money and the club needs you."

"How do you know I need money?" she asked, a sinking feeling in her stomach. Granted, she had grabbed the money quickly the night before, but she had hoped desperation wasn't completely apparent on her face.

Intimidation was the only thing that would make her do it at this point, and he knew it.

"There's nothing the club doesn't know about you. I know your house is in foreclosure. I know that you're having a hard time feeding your children. I'm offering you a way out. Do this for them if you won't do it for anyone else."

His words were completely below the belt, but they were also completely true. "Promise me that my kids won't be hurt."

That was the one thing he *could* promise her. The children would not be hurt on his watch.

"I can promise you. I will protect them with my life."

Taking a deep breath, she closed her eyes.

"Tell me where and when."

The deal was made, and she knew that she wouldn't be able to back out. If she backed out, she knew without a doubt he *wouldn't* be able to protect her children. Just like everything else in her life up to this point, she would do it for them. That would help her sleep at night.

Chapter Three

"I'm fucked," she said out loud. No one was there to hear her or to see her break down, but for the first time since this had started, she sobbed. Really sobbed. It was full body and it was ugly.

Denise sat on her couch, her head in her hands. The last year and a half had taught her many things about herself and about life. She had come to some grim realizations and some new revelations.

She wasn't as strong as she had once believed. When she had been a teenager having twins, she had taken the world by the balls and dared it to talk back to her. This time, when the economy had tanked and she had lost her job, she had cowered. For months she had sat on her living room couch, just knowing the factory would call her back and tell her to come to work on Monday morning. When that hadn't happened, it had taken her a few weeks, but she dove headlong into looking for something else. It had taken months for her to find the minimum wage job she now worked at. Gone were most of their DVD's and any jewelry she'd had. Lately she'd taken to switching coins out of the cash registers at work, getting the oldest coins she could in order to take them downtown and sell them to the local coin store. That wasn't getting her very far now that her hours at work had been cut.

In the middle of her complete freak out, she heard a knock at her door and she tensed. The last three times someone had knocked on her door, it had been a disaster. She wondered if she should just act like she wasn't home. Maybe the person on the other side would just leave.

"Denise, I know you're in there."

It was her neighbor from up the street. Meredith Rager, the local television reporter. They had become acquaintances, perhaps friends lately, and Denise really didn't want to be alone anymore.

"Coming," she coughed, struggling to disguise the pinched tone of her voice. Mopping up her cheeks, she opened the door.

"Hey, I saw Liam Walker leaving here," Meredith started before getting a good look at Denise's face. "Did he hurt you?" she asked, sharply.

"He didn't hurt me."

"Are you sure?" Meredith asked, walking into the house. "I've dealt with these guys a couple of times when I interviewed them in front of the jail. They aren't nice people. I'm pretty sure they all have a little bit of blood on their hands."

"I'm sure. He really didn't hurt me. He was actually nicer than he probably needed to be."

Immediately, Meredith's radar was buzzing. What else had Liam Walker been doing at Denise Cunningham's house? "You're not getting involved with them are you?"

Denise didn't want to get into this. Meredith was very astute, and Denise was an open book. Calling upon those feelings that had made her so emotional earlier, Denise scrunched her face up and let a sob break through her chest.

"What's happened?" the other woman asked, worried about the single mother.

Reaching under the couch cushion, she pulled out the foreclosure paperwork. "I got served with these yesterday, and I just don't know what to do anymore."

Grabbing the papers from Denise's hand, Meredith looked over it, her eyebrows drawing together in concentration. "Shit," she breathed. "This amount isn't going to be easy to come up with."

"I know," Denise cried. Usually she wouldn't be putting her business out there for just anyone to know, but besides Roni, Meredith was the only friend Denise had at this point. "I just don't know what I'm going to do. This is the only home my children have ever known, and now they're going to lose it."

Meredith's heart ached. She had grown up in a family where money wasn't an issue. It wasn't like they were extravagantly wealthy, but there had never been a week where they had to order off the dollar menu because they weren't able to afford food. This was not her reality, and she wasn't familiar with it, but she could at least be sympathetic.

"Do you want me to give you money?" Meredith asked. She didn't have the amount that Denise needed, but maybe she had enough to keep the wolves at bay.

That caused tears to come faster and sobs to wrack Denise's body harder. She had never had anyone she could count on or ask for money when she needed it. This was one of the nicest things anyone had ever said to her.

"I truly appreciate it, but I can't take your money. I'm serious when I say I probably will never be able to pay you back, and that just makes me uncomfortable."

Meredith's eyebrows drew together. "That's why Liam was here, right?" This time her tone didn't carry the question that it had earlier. This time she knew. Desperate people did desperate things, and Denise was the epitome of desperate.

"I'd really rather not talk about it."

"Okay, let's head over to my duplex and have some lunch before I have to go to work. You need to get out of this house. If you sit here, you're just going to think of things you can't control."

Denise knew she was right. She *was* hungry, and she had next to no food in the house. "That sounds great."

"Did you convince her to help us?" William asked his son as Liam pulled his bike up in front of *Walker's Wheels* and shut it off.

The shop provided legitimate income for the club, and everyone was expected to put time in there. They did everything from oil changes to repos and towing.

Before he took his helmet off, Liam looked around at the activity bustling around them. It was at moments like this when he wished he was exactly what he looked like. A son helping out his father at the family business. Business was booming, and every extra hand they had was busy – either changing oil or doing bodywork.

"What do I need to do today?" Liam asked, ignoring his dad's question.

"You need to tell me if Denise is goin' to help us or not."

"That's not what I'm talkin' about, and you know it. If Denise is going to work with us, she's going to work under me. You'll know what the fuck's goin' on – on a need to know basis. Now what the fuck do I need to do to help out here today?" His tone said there would be no arguing.

William cut his eyes to Liam, not happy with the way this conversation was going. "There's two bikes that need oil changes, and then I need you to check the car that we're sending with Denise tomorrow."

"Will do, Dad."

Liam sauntered off, grabbing Tyler away from the job he was working on to go under the hood of a late model avocado green Cutlass Supreme.

"Whose car is this?" Tyler asked. He hadn't seen it on the work order for the day.

Throwing a glare at William, Liam answered. "This is the car that we need to take to Denise's tonight."

"She agreed to it? I thought she was smarter than that."

"I did too, but she's desperate. You and I both know that desperation can make you do stupid shit. We count on that to get the things we want in this club. It sucks a big one when that's used against people it shouldn't be."

It was on the tip of Tyler's tongue to say that desperation really shouldn't ever be used against anyone – no matter who they were. But the club was the club, and they did things the way they had to in order to get what they wanted. He could understand where Liam was coming from though. This woman wasn't a hardened criminal, she didn't even want to do this to get in good with any of the Brothers. On top of that, she had absolutely zero experience. This would either be the best plan they had ever had, or it would blow completely up in their faces. He just hoped no one got hurt.

"Thanks for lunch, Meredith. You were right, I really did need to get out of that house," Denise said as she walked to the front door of Meredith's duplex.

"Glad I could be of help," she smiled. "I hate to kick you out, but I have to get ready to do the news in a few hours. I still haven't gotten the script going yet either."

Meredith was the usual anchor at 6 o'clock, but she really wanted the 10 o'clock or early morning job. Those were the most prestigious in this small town. Tonight she'd had to switch in order to cover the later shift, and she planned on making it count.

"Good luck." Denise told her as she walked out onto Meredith's porch and then the short way up the street to where her house sat.

There on the front door was a yellow tag. Not sure what it was, she grabbed it and flipped it over. It told her to call the Sherriff's Office. It didn't take a scientist to figure out that everything she had been running from was catching up to her at warp speed. She had to do this job, and it had to be now. For her survival and the survival of her children, this had to happen.

Chapter Four

A car was parked in your driveway during the night with keys located in the visor. Once you get in the car, plug in the GPS. Follow the directions, and it will tell you where to go. After the drop is made, someone from the club will pick you up. Further instructions await you at your destination.

Denise read the text message again to make sure she understood what it was saying. Last night before Liam left, he provided her with a pre-paid cell phone and told her to wait for someone to contact her. With stunning realization, the fact that she was about to break the law hit her. Never in her life had she broken the law.

"Why am I doing this?" she whispered as she glanced around her kitchen.

A stack of unpaid bills caught her attention where they lay on the counter. Beside them sat open house fliers for her kids. If she didn't do this job, there would be no clothes for school, no supplies. They would be forced once again to go to the resources office. Denise knew that the other kids made fun of those who needed financial help. The twins had already had to put up with that last year, she didn't want them to have to go through that again. The answer stared back at her. Squaring her shoulders, Denise realized there was no time like the present to make the change from law abiding citizen to biker gang lackey.

She hadn't been sure what to expect when she shut and locked the front door to her home, but the car in her driveway wasn't it. A late model Cutlass Supreme, avocado green in color, sat behind her little four door sedan. It reminded her of the cars that so many young people were beginning to fix up as classics from the early 1980s. Walking over, she got in and opened the visor. Sure enough, keys fell into her lap. A GPS was already mounted on the dashboard, and all she had to do was plug it into a modified cigarette lighter. Turning it on, she waited for it to find all its satellites and then listened as it instructed her to turn left out of the driveway. She took a deep breath and steeled herself. A car this old was bound to be loud and draw a lot of attention. When it started up, however, she couldn't even tell it was running until she gave it a little gas.

As she made her way out of her neighborhood, she wondered just exactly what was in this car. What kind of drugs was she transporting, and how much time could she get for it if she were to be caught?

A few minutes later, Denise was merging west onto the William Natcher Parkway in order to head north towards Owensboro. She had made this drive many times in the past. With Bowling Green being centrally located, she often took trips to Owensboro, Louisville, or Nashville. This time however, she was nervous. Even though this stretch of road wasn't usually monitored by the police, she found herself checking her side and rearview mirrors almost obsessively. Her hands gripped the steering wheel much harder than they had to, and she could feel the tension in her shoulders as the car ate up the miles.

The closer she got to Owensboro, the more her stomach churned. Listening intently, she waited to see where the GPS would tell her to go next. Following its instructions, she turned onto West Petit Road until she came across a set of train tracks with a house located in front of them. The driving directions seemed to end at the house. Her mind ran a million miles a minute with the many scenarios that could happen here. Was someone going to kidnap her? Hurt her? Hold her for ransom?

Awareness pricked on the back of her neck. Without seeing them, she knew that others watched her. Not sure what to do, she pulled next to the house and waited. Once the GPS registered that she had reached her destination, a message popped up on the GPS that told her to leave the car where it was and wait to be picked up. She didn't realized how hot she was until she got out of the car. Sweat clung to the nape of her neck, and she felt as if the world was closing in on her. Stepping further from the house, she sought out the breeze that would surely be blowing. If she wasn't mistaken, this land bordered a creek and perhaps the coolness would be flowing off of it.

It was at least 15 degrees cooler closer to the creek. For the first time she noticed her surroundings. She was out in the middle of nowhere, and had she needed help there would be no one who could do that. Just as she began to panic, she heard the steady hum of a motorcycle. With no place to hide, she stood out in in the open, hoping this was friend and not foe. As the bike got closer, she realized it was Liam. Her heart sped up when he came to a stop in front of her, killing the engine.

"I'm your ride. Did you have any issues getting out here?"

Her mouth went dry when he took off his helmet and hung it on the handlebars. There was something about this man on a bike. It was as if he were at home. The bike and he were made to fit one another. The jeans he wore hugged his thighs just so, and the white t-shirt under his cut showed off a tan that came from many hours of riding. To keep from having to stare into his eyes, she looked down, noticing the motorcycle boots that encased his feet. They looked like they could kick a hole in someone, and it made her shiver.

"No problems at all. I was just a little lost when I got here until I noticed the GPS had flashed to another screen."

"Good," he smiled and she noticed just how straight and white his teeth were. She wondered if all young bikers looked like this or if he was just special. "We need to be movin'. The pick-up crew should be here in a few minutes, and we don't wanna be around to see them."

"You want me to ride that?" she asked, looking around. Maybe he would produce a car out of thin air.

He grinned, cocking an eyebrow. "I do own a truck, maybe I shoulda drove that? This is easier to maneuver though."

"You think we're gonna have to maneuver?"

"When dealin' with us, you never know." She appreciated that he was honest, but it didn't make her feel any better about this situation.

At that moment they heard the roar of motorcycles, lots of them. "That's not our contact here in Owensboro, we need to get outta here."

"How do you know?" she asked. To her it was amazing that someone could differentiate motorcycles based on sound alone.

"Those are European bikes. You can tell by the volume of the rumble. It's probably the Vojnik."

"The who?" she asked, hopping on behind him and grabbing him securely around the waist.

"Bosnian for soldier. They are the local Bosnian biker gang, we ain't exactly friendly. They're probably trying to steal the shipment," he flashed her what could only described as a bad boy smile. "We stole one of theirs last week."

He peeled out, gravel spitting behind them as he took to the main road. Denise had been on a motorcycle maybe two times in her life, but it had never been like this.

"Hold on tight," he yelled behind him.

She gripped her fingers into the leather he wore around his waist and held on for dear life. Behind her, she could hear the bikes gaining on them. Apparently though, Liam was familiar with this section of road. He turned onto a path that she hadn't even seen and proceeded to drive them across a field. Few of the other bikers made the hairpin turn and by the time they did, she and Liam were far ahead. Shots were fired. She screamed as they buzzed her head.

A few miles down the road, they came to a complete stop and he shut the bike off. "You okay?"

Adrenaline and fear bubbled up in her throat, building on everything she had been through, before she took a swing at him, connecting with his chin. "Are you fucking crazy? You got me shot at!"

He blocked her next punches and held her arms at her sides. "If I let you go, are you gonna take another swing at me?" Damn, but she had a wicked hook. He had to shake his head momentarily because she had knocked him loopy.

She sagged in his arms, the rush leaving her. To her horror she started shaking, and her teeth chattered. "I won't swing at you again. You have my word."

Letting her go, he pulled her into his arms, rubbing the shakes out of her body. "Just let it flow through you. It's the adrenaline."

"Why do people *want* to do this?" she asked, her voice wobbly, showing her true feelings about her new endeavor. She wasn't cut out for this, that much was apparent.

"It's all some people know. Some of us were born into this, whether we wanted to be or not." His voice was low and raw with emotion.

That made her sad. It was obvious that Liam had never had another option. She wanted to give her children a different option. To not live hand to mouth and to not live worrying about how they would pay their electric bill. Seeing the empty feeling in his eyes convinced her that she was doing this for all the right reasons.

Hours later, Denise sat at the dinner table with her children. For the first time in months, she'd had money to go out and get steak. Her son, Andrew, grilled them while her daughter, Amanda, baked potatoes. Denise put the fear of her earlier brush with death behind her and made a salad. Talk at the table had been animated, much like any conversation with thirteen-year-old twins would be. She realized watching them make dinner how much older they acted now. It was obvious they'd had to take care of themselves much more than she would have liked.

"This is good, Mom," Andrew praised, wiping his mouth with a napkin. His table manners made her proud.

"Thanks, but it was you at the grill who did most of the work," she smiled at him.

Each day, he made the move further into manhood. His face had already lost the boyish features of innocence. A small mustache was beginning to form on his upper lip. Would she be able to move him into young adulthood? Those fears plagued her at night just as much as her money situation did. Somehow, she knew that she had to make things right. Her family counted on it.

Chapter Five

"I'm telling you, there have been some huge deposits lately. One of them is striking me as odd."

Meredith quirked her brow and put her phone in between her ear and shoulder. Picking up a pen, she poised it to take down the information from her contact at the most prominent bank in town. For months she had been watching large deposits come in for numerous people. She had begun working on tracing the money back, and she was finding a pattern. Most went back to judges, police, sheriffs, and members of the city council, others went to just your normal run of the mill citizen. She knew that most of this was for the Heaven Hill club. They had to be paying people to do their dirty work. If there was a new development, it could break this wide open.

"Who is it?"

"Denise Cunningham and let me tell ya how odd this is. She's been in the red for over a year. Not too long ago her account was frozen by a creditor, and they couldn't even get any money out of it. That's how broke she's been. This morning, she made a $15,000 cash deposit. Tell me where she got that money."

Her mouth went dry. A journalist's mind worked fast, and Meredith's was no exception. She flashed back to the day before, the green, late model Cutlass sitting in Denise's driveway, the conversation the two of them had, and Liam seen leaving Denise's house. Everything was beginning to point in one direction for Meredith - Heaven Hill.

"Thanks for the info. You don't know how much this has helped me."

"Remember Meredith, this is illegal. No one can know I'm helping you. We have to keep this between us. I could lose everything."

She rolled her eyes. Every time they did this she always got the same reminder. "We've been doing this for months. I think I know what I'm doing."

"Just so we're clear."

"We are. I gotta go."

Hanging up the phone, Meredith walked back to her bedroom window and peeked through the curtain at Denise's driveway. Denise's car sat in its normal spot. Refusing to let this one go, Meredith grabbed her keys and marched out of her house, intent on finding out just what the hell was going on.

It scared her, really, the fact that they had decided to prey on her friend, and now she appeared to be in Heaven Hill's pocket. Denise was *not* a criminal, and Meredith didn't want to see her go down this road.

Denise glanced at herself in the mirror. The stress of the previous year had really done a number on her. She had lost weight and it showed. Her eyes looked tired, and she'd found a gray hair the other day. It didn't escape her that she looked a little bit older than her years. The new clothes she'd bought helped that. On a whim, she'd taken a small amount of her money and gone to the mall. For the first time in years she'd bought new clothes. It was kind of exciting to discover she was two sizes smaller. It reminded her that she hadn't acted her age in a very long time and that she needed just a little bit of fun in her life. It felt strange thinking of that when all she'd done lately was worry about money and bills. She was finally thinking like a woman her age.

A loud banging at her front door caused her to jump. It reminded her of the sheriff the other day. Thank God this was the first day of school and the kids weren't home.

Walking over, she looked through the storm door. A smile appeared on her face as she saw Meredith through the window. Opening it up, she stepped out. "Hey."

Meredith regarded her with cool eyes. "We should talk about this inside."

"Then please come in."

The two of them went inside, and Meredith gazed around. It looked just like it had the day before. The living room was clean, furniture was old but well cared for. It was obvious the carpet needed replacing but it too was clean. This was not the home of someone who fraternized with the likes of a gang like Heaven Hill or even someone who recently obtained a large amount of money. She wasn't sure what she had expected – a brand new TV and game system maybe?

"What the hell do you think you're doing?" Meredith blurted.

Arms crossed over her chest, Denise sucked in a breath. "Excuse me?"

"Working with that gang of thugs."

"What are you talking about?" She tried to play dumb, like they just hadn't danced around this conversation the day before.

Her smile evil, Meredith ran her tongue over her teeth. "You know exactly what I'm talking about. I saw that car in your driveway yesterday. I saw the GPS attached to it. Why did a piece of shit like that need a GPS? I saw *you* get in it and drive away, so don't tell me you had company either. Why are you working with Heaven Hill?"

Rage flew through Denise. Why wouldn't they all just leave her alone? She was damn tired of everyone using her for their own agenda. The feelings she'd had the day before about not wanting Meredith to know the extent she was working for Heaven Hill were back and she reacted with anger.

"Get out!"

"I'm telling you that these people are bad, Denise. Do you really want them around your kids? Think about them."

"I am," she screamed. All the rage and fear began to manifest again. "I *am* thinking about them. If I didn't do what I had to, they would go hungry tonight. They wouldn't have food. They wouldn't have a home to live in. Would you rather us be homeless and out on the street?"

She paced back and forth, her rage threatening to consume her.

"Have you ever been in my shoes? I've made choices that I never should have had to make because of an economy that doesn't care about the working class. I've had to make decisions because of situations that are completely out of my control. I never expected to have twins at the age I did, and I sure as hell never expected their father to leave me. I have done what I can with the circumstances I have been given. No one asked if you agreed with it. I don't recall asking you anything at all."

She took a deep breath and marched to the front door. Opening it, she held it for her.

"Get the hell out of my house. I will not be a pawn in your game to get this gang. You want them? You get them yourself. We're friends, but I *cannot* help you with this."

Meredith walked out the door knowing she would get nothing more out of Denise. The slam of the door echoed loudly behind her. Meredith stood there shocked, but she wouldn't be deterred. If there was one thing she knew, it was how to flip others to her way of thinking. She would break this story if it was the last thing she did.

"What do you mean a reporter is asking questions?" Roni asked as she sat in the clubhouse talking on her cell phone.

Liam's ears perked as he heard her words. This could be trouble, depending on who she was talking to on the other end of the line.

"Let me talk to my brother, and I'll get back to you."

He took a sip of his beer and leaned back in his chair, eyebrows raised in question. "Who was that? Something we need to take care of?"

"That was Denise. That damn reporter has already sniffed her out."

On the other side of the clubhouse, William inhaled from his cigar and waited to see what his offspring were going to say. "You still questioning my authority?"

"No, I'm questioning your common sense. Who in their right mind decides that a single mother who is having financial issues is ready for all of this? We threw her to the goddamned wolves. We need to get to her before that Rager bitch goes to the police. You know she'll probably run something tonight. This is more our fault than anyone else's. She wasn't ready for this, and we were reckless."

Liam watched as his father took another long draw off his cigar. "Bring her here. We need to find out what she said to the reporter."

"At this point, I'm not sure she'll have anything to do with us," Liam muttered.

"She doesn't have a choice."

Denise sighed as she heard the motorcycle pull into her driveway. She figured that across the street Meredith was probably taking pictures. Hell, she'd probably bugged her home when she'd been there earlier. They had been on their way to such a good friendship too. She was going to miss that.

Liam walked in without even knocking.

"I didn't know we were that comfortable with each other," she dryly greeted him. "You know, for you just to walk into my house."

"Get your stuff and get your kids from school, we gotta go."

She could tell by the look on his face and the tone of his voice he meant business.

"Am I in trouble? Are you going to kill me?"

He saw her lower lip tremble and wanted to kill his father. "No we aren't going to kill you, but we all need to be clear about what's going on here. I promised you that your kids would be fine, and I keep my promises."

She noted that he had never promised she would be fine. She was now at the mercy of these people, and it was very clear that she was in way over her head.

Chapter Six

"Momma, where are we goin'?"

Denise sighed. It was moments like these that she wished there was someone else to help answer the children's questions. "To a friend's house, Mandy. Like I've already told you three times."

Her patience was beginning to run thin. She had no idea where Liam was taking her, only knew it was her job to follow. Gripping the steering wheel, she thought back on the choices she had made. No matter what happened here this afternoon, they had been the right ones. The only ones she felt that she could make. It wouldn't do to second guess herself now.

"We don't know anybody who lives out here," Mandy argued.

"Amanda Cunningham, I'm going to say this one time and one time only. We are going to a friend's house, and if you open your mouth again you'll wish you hadn't."

Properly scolded, Mandy sat back in her seat and began picking at the nail polish on her fingers. Every once in a while, she glanced up at her mother in the rearview mirror and rolled her eyes.

"You're pushin' it, little girl."

It struck her at that moment – the differences in her children. Mandy back talked when she was scared and wanted to know exactly what was going on. Drew, on the other hand, reminded her a lot of Liam. He sat with his eyes straight ahead, taking in their surroundings. She could almost see his mind working through all of this, and she had a sneaking suspicion her son knew it all.

Liam had gotten further ahead of them on the road as the battle of wills with her daughter ensued. Denise pressed the accelerator to catch up. She questioned why she suddenly seemed so willing to follow him anywhere he might lead her. As far as she was concerned, he was as much to blame for this as she was. As they traveled down Porter Pike, he took her further out in to the county than she had ever been before. They passed a volunteer fire department, and she noticed a highway number. If she wasn't mistaken, they weren't too far away from the eastern boundary of the county. Up ahead, his brake lights flickered, and he pulled onto a gravel road. Signaling, she followed him, and they drove for what seemed like miles before they crested a hill. There sat the largest garage-like building she'd ever seen, surrounded by motorcycles.

"Mom? When did these people become your friends?" Drew asked, his mouth agape at the scene.

"I'll tell you just like I told your sister. Hush."

Liam parked his bike beside those that lined the drive and motioned for her to park her car. Her heart pounded as she put the car in park and instructed the kids to get out.

"They can go hang out with Roni. She usually keeps the kids preoccupied." He pointed to where Roni stood observing a group of kids playing basketball and riding bikes.

"I'm not leaving my mom alone with you," Drew lifted his chin in defiance.

Liam respected what the boy was trying to do but knew that he couldn't let him get in the way. He stepped in front of Denise and put his hands on the boy's shoulders.

"We need to take care of some adult business."

The two males sized one another up. Finally, Drew gave in and followed his sister to where the other kids hung out.

"Let's get inside. William wants to talk to you."

It might have been false, but she felt a sense of protection as she walked in with Liam at her side. He placed a hand at the small of her back, leading her into the main room of the clubhouse. It was dark to her, miscellaneous posters hung on the walls along with pictures of different men. She assumed they had something do with the history of the club, but she really didn't know. A row of couches sat in the corner, a pool table beside them. In the other corner, a large table had been set up that was obviously used as a kitchen table, and there were a group of recliners. It looked comfortable, but not at all welcoming. Conversation ceased when they arrived. Liam watched, his eyes taking in everything as his father walked over to where they stood. He didn't like the look in the older man's eyes.

"I take it you're Denise?"

Shyly, she nodded. This man's demeanor was completely different than the younger one standing next to her. That could be seen by the tick in his jaw as he looked at her. He didn't have a relaxed air about him like Liam did. This man *wanted* to intimidate her.

"What did that reporter want with you?" he asked gruffly. She knew that his tone of voice was meant to scare her, but instead it made her angry.

"She wants to use me to get to you. Somehow she knows that you've recruited me."

His face flushed red. "Well then you must have told her"

"I didn't tell anyone anything. *She* came to *me!*" Her voice shook with fear and anger. She didn't appreciate being put in this situation.

This wasn't going to end well, Liam could tell. Emotions were running high, Denise was scared to death, and William was pissed beyond belief. Neither one of them appeared to want to listen to what the other had to say.

"And just how did she know to come to you?" he questioned.

She wanted to cry. Throwing her hands up in the air, she just said, "I don't know."

"You did one job for us and she's already on to you?"

"I don't know how."

"What did you say to her to give yourself away?"

"I don't know." she screamed. "I didn't talk to her about this. I am just a single mother minding my own business, *you* came to *me*. Not the other way around."

William Walker did not allow anyone to yell at him. Denise, in her frustration, was beginning to get louder. Liam stepped forward and placed a hand on her shoulder. Irritated, she shrugged it off.

"I'd watch your tone if I was you," William warned her, sticking a finger in her face.

"If you were me, you wouldn't be in this situation. I got bullied by *you* to do a job that you knew would put a bull's-eye on my back. If you're wondering how she knew about me, maybe you should look at your own people. They are the only people who knew about it."

"Are you tellin' me you think my people have loose lips?"

She crossed her arms over her chest, put off by the questions being asked. "I think you know exactly what I'm saying."

Without warning, the bigger man leaned back and clocked her across the face. With a gasp, she fell to the floor, holding her cheek. Blood poured from her nose, and her cheek started to bruise almost immediately. Liam reached down to help her up. He shook with fury, none of them liked to see women hurt, and he had told this one's son that she wouldn't be. In the span of minutes, he'd managed to break a promise. That was just great, and his own father was the one to thank for that. Sometimes he wished they didn't share the same name or the same blood.

"Was that really necessary, Dad?"

"She questioned me and this club. We all know the rules here."

"Yeah, but *she* doesn't."

"Are you starting to question me now? I'll do ten times worse to you."

Liam swallowed hard. He knew what was coming if he dared say the things he wanted to. He felt that most of this was his fault. Had he spoken up louder, sooner, maybe he could have kept her from this. Now was the time to take the stand he hadn't taken before.

"I'm not questioning you. I'm *telling* you if you touch her again, you'll deal with me."

Shock was evident on William's face as the words came out of his son's mouth. "You do realize what you're saying, right?"

"I do. This won't be happening here, Dad. You won't be touching her again."

Denise wondered just what in the hell he meant. This time, however, she did leave her mouth shut. The Native American, whom she recognized from the news as the one arrested with Liam, approached them and pressed a towel to her face. It must have held ice because it felt blessedly cool.

"In case anyone missed what went down here, this woman is now my property," Liam announced loudly. "You got something to say? You say it to me," he looked directly in his father's eyes as he spoke.

Denise wanted to scream at him. She, out of everyone, had missed what went down. She didn't know what being his property entailed, and she sure as hell didn't want to find out right this instant.

The crowd was silent as the two of them left, Tyler watching their backs as they exited the building. Once outside, Denise yelled for the kids. Disappointment and fear was plain on Andrew's face as he looked from Liam to his mom.

"Who hit her?" he demanded.

Realizing for the first time just how dangerous this situation could be, Denise herded him to the car along with Mandy as she threw the towel down on the ground. She wanted absolutely nothing to remind her of this place. Not even waiting for Liam, she got in her car and drove off as fast as she could. The kids screamed questions at her as her car kicked up dust in her wake.

"Damnit!"

Liam knew he couldn't leave her alone. He had claimed her now in front of everyone. She was his property, whether she wanted to be or not.

Chapter Seven

"You better go after her."

Liam glared at his sister as she walked over to stand with beside him. Nothing about any of this was easy, and he didn't want to hear other people's opinions.

"She obviously wants nothing to do with me or us." He blew out a breath and ran a hand through his dark hair.

"That's not just her decision anymore, and you know it. You've claimed her, and she's been seen with you. Our enemies will be after her and her family now. I feel horrible about this," she whispered. She had always been the worrier of the two of them. Above all, Roni tried to be a good person, and he knew hurting Denise would be tearing her up.

He slung his arm over her shoulder and brought her close to his body. "You didn't mean for this to happen any more than I did. It was our bastard of a father. Unfortunately, we can't say no to him."

Truer words had never been spoken, and it wasn't the first time that Roni wished their mother was around. She would never speak those words to anyone, but at times like these they needed an ally.

"No, but we should have looked out for her and her kids. What's gonna happen now? What kinda danger is she going to be in because of us?"

Squaring his shoulders, he turned her to face him. "Nothin' is going to happen to that family again. I've promised my protection and that's what they will have."

"What if she doesn't want it?"

"I think it's pretty goddamn obvious she doesn't want it, but she doesn't have a choice. What I want, I get."

Roni knew he spoke the truth. He always got what he wanted, but he did it in a much better way than their father.

"Anybody ever tell you what an asshole you are?"

William turned sharply to face the voice of his estranged wife, Lauren. Neither Liam nor Roni knew she still came to the club, but the two of them couldn't seem to stay away from each other. There was absolute love there, but they couldn't deal with one another on a day to day basis. Liam didn't trust her, so they kept most of their meetings private.

"You, on more than one occasion."

Damn, he missed her being here all the time. When he had started this club, it had been for her, it had been for his family. When they got too deep in the illegal activities, she ran. Abandoning her children, but not abandoning her feelings for him.

"I think right now I have to be honest with you. You're driving him away, and you need to watch it before you push him so far he doesn't come back. Just like I did."

"I'm trying to teach him to be a leader," he explained gruffly.

Lauren put her hand on her husband's shoulder. "What's more important? Him being a good leader or being your son? The two of you are in a very dangerous situation, and you are walking a tightrope. He only has one father, and you only have one son." She was careful with the words she used; it wouldn't serve any purpose to get William mad at her. "Don't let a sense of loyalty to the club disrupt that. Liam is a damn good man. These younger guys follow him first and ask questions later because of his heart and his loyalty. Don't perceive it as a threat, allow him to grow. Don't break him the way I did. I know what I did was wrong, but it's too late to go back and change that now."

William could see the decisions she had made were weighing on her. If he had been a better man, he would have offered her his shoulder and told her that no matter what Liam was still her son and would love her unconditionally. But he wasn't that man.

"You're right. He hates you, and that's never gonna change."

She took a deep breath, her heart sinking at those words. He was right, and she wasn't sure she could ever make that change.

"Get upstairs and do your homework."

"We don't have any, school just started," Drew reminded her before she pinned him with a look. It wasn't long before she heard feet running quickly up the stairs, almost as if they couldn't get away from her fast enough. Bedroom doors slammed, and at last she was alone. Sinking to the couch, she put her head in her hands.

"What the ever-loving-fuck have I done?" she asked herself out loud.

The phone rang at her side, and she laughed as she recognized the number. It was her job, probably calling her in on her day off. She should have been happy with that job, and she wouldn't be in this situation now. The ringing grated her nerves and she reached over, sending it to voicemail.

"What am I going to do?"

She had a little bit of money left from the club. Paying off the credit cards and house had taken most of it, but she could just let the bank take the house. She and the kids could run a long way on the money she had made. They had been frugal for the past year, they could learn to be even more so. She could homeschool, and they could start a new life somewhere different, somewhere this bad luck didn't seem to follow her. The only family she really had was upstairs, and possessions didn't matter if they weren't alive to enjoy them. She could pack what they needed tonight, and then go to the bank tomorrow morning to withdraw all the remaining money. They could be miles from town before noon.

Mind made up, she ran for the bedroom and grabbed a suitcase. She threw clothes inside, trying to keep her panic at bay. At this moment it felt like they were running for their lives. The roar of a motorcycle interrupted her thoughts and gave her pause. She missed the time – was it only a few short days ago? – when the roar of a motorcycle meant nothing to her. If Liam was here to talk her into something, he was sorely mistaken. She wasn't stupid, and she wouldn't be making the same mistake twice. Bracing herself for the knock she knew was coming, she tried to even out her breathing and calm down her temper. She'd finally reached the 'lose my shit' point and she was ready to let him have it.

Without warning the window of her bedroom shattered, broken glass raining down on her. Almost instinctively she dropped to the floor. She could feel pricks at her scalp and knew she was bleeding. Taking stock of what had happened, she gazed around the bedroom. There on the floor not five feet from her lay a brick.

"Mom, are you okay?" both kids asked breathlessly as they stood in the doorway to her bedroom.

"I'm fine." She winced as her fingers felt her scalp.

The front door slammed shut causing all of them to swivel round on alert. Liam stalked through, rage on his face.

"Is everybody okay in here?"

Drew lost it when he saw the man, running at him with a loud war cry. He caught Liam around the waist, bringing them both to the ground. Once the boy was on top of him, Drew began swinging. Mandy and Denise were screaming at the two of them without trying to intervene. Denise was afraid to get up because she didn't know where glass was lodged, and Mandy was afraid she was going to get hit in the melee.

"Andrew. Get off of him now." Denise yelled.

The boy just kept hitting the man, Liam grunting as Drew made contact with muscle and flesh. Finally Liam was able to flip them over and hold his arms down over Drew's. "You done?" he asked, afraid to let him go.

Drew's body heaved as he tried to control his breathing. It had taken almost everything out of him as he tried to purge the anger he had towards Liam.

"Answer me. You done?"

Tears streamed down the teenager's face as he nodded.

"Now, are you two okay?" Liam again asked, wiping blood from his lip and nose.

"I'm fine," Mandy whispered, in shock over what she had just witnessed.

"I'm good too, but I just don't know where all this glass is. They aren't wearing shoes, and I don't want to track it everywhere. I know I've got some cuts, but I don't think any are deep."

He took in the state of the bedroom and glared at her. "Going somewhere?"

"Why don't the two of you go upstairs and work on your rooms while I clean up this mess."

They watched as the twins reluctantly walked upstairs. Once they were gone, Liam turned to face her.

"Again. Going somewhere?"

He helped her get up from the floor, brushing glass away from her. She didn't have shoes on, so he carried her over to a chair in the corner.

"It's really none of your business if I am," she said flippantly.

"Oh, that's where I beg to differ, sweetheart. Where's your broom?"

She pointed towards the kitchen and watched as he came back with the broom and dustpan. Without even asking, he began sweeping, still talking.

"I've put my protection on you. In the grand scheme of the club we may as well be married. The Vojnik have seen you with me too, so we need to get you and the kids out of here. That's probably what this business is about," he gestured at the dustpan.

It didn't sit well with her that all her decisions were being made for her. "We're not leaving our home."

"The hell you're not, you were planning on leaving anyway. Why not leave with me?"

"Should I really count the reasons? I don't know you, I don't trust you, and I'm not even sure I *like* you."

Finished sweeping up the glass, he leaned over and grabbed the brick that had come through the window. Rolling it over in his hands, he held it out to her.

"This is another reason you should want to be with me. I can protect you from this."

"You're the *reason* for this," she argued. Taking the brick from him, she flipped it over in her hands. Foreign words were written on it, and she didn't know how to make heads or tails of what it said.

"What is this?"

"A threat from the Vojnik. They saw you with me, and they'll assume you're an easy way to get to me. Your only choice is to come with me."

This was a hard pill to swallow. Before he'd showed up, she'd had a plan. A plan she felt good about. A way to get out of this mess. That was now all gone. Feeling defeated, she nodded. Getting up, she called for the kids, telling them to pack some bags as she did the same. Who would have thought covering a simple shift at work would have ever led to all of this.

"Can you tell your sister that the next time she needs me to cover her shift – she's shit out of luck?"

For the first time, she heard him laugh, and a genuine smile transformed his face. She knew with everything in her that she *did* need protection but of a different kind than he was offering. She needed protection from him.

Chapter Eight

Meredith sat in the same chair she had been sitting in for hours. Overnight and into early morning, she had watched Denise all but move out. Liam Walker and a few other members of Heaven Hill were loading suitcases into Denise's car and standing around looking menacing. Tyler Blackfoot, the best friend and handsome Native American, had stalked like a shadow watching over the group. What had happened? Was Denise an old lady now? It was obvious that Liam had offered protection of some sort, otherwise the club wouldn't have had a show of force like that. Did the window the men had boarded up figure into any of this?

"What am I missing?" she questioned herself, biting the nail of her index finger.

She wanted to expose the illegal activities of the club. That kind of story would do amazing things for her career. And it would get part of the criminal element out of Bowling Green. The last thing she wanted to do was ruin what had become a friendship with Denise. However, in her heart she knew that Denise was the key to breaking them. Meredith didn't want to use her, but realized she would if she had to. That didn't sit well with her, never in her career had she used someone she was close with. She could almost taste the praise that her boss would give her, and she craved that approval. It just didn't feel as victorious as she had assumed it would.

The last motorcycle and Denise's car had left roughly forty five minutes before. Maybe she could go look around, see if they had left any clues. She put on her running shoes and grabbed her iPhone before walking out the door. She stopped in her driveway to stretch like she normally did before a run and then casually jogged down the street. As she got to Denise's house, she walked up the front porch and tried the door.

"Son of a bitch, they left it unlocked," she breathed, glancing around to make sure no one was watching.

Once inside, she let her eyes adjust to the darkness before scanning the room. It was obvious that they had left in a hurry but care had also been used to pack certain things. She made her way to the room where the window had been boarded up. On the dresser in the corner she found a brick with Bosnian writing on it.

"Bingo."

She couldn't read Bosnian but knew a few people who could. Using her iPhone, she took pictures of it from different angles as well as a picture of the window that it had obviously come through.

"I don't think so." The voice was deep and authoritative with a slight southern accent that caused her skin to prickle with awareness.

It belonged to Tyler Blackfoot. He wasn't supposed to be here, there were no bikes outside. She turned around, hand on her hip. "What are you doing here?"

"I could ask you the same question. Give me the phone," he motioned with his hand. The man was larger than life and beautiful really, but right now he was annoying her.

"I live in the neighborhood, I was worried."

He smirked, white teeth showing against his tan skin. "But you don't live in this house do you? Give me the phone," he said again.

"It's my property."

"And you are trespassing. Do you know how much I'd love to call the cops on you and then take *your* picture as you come out of jail?"

Her eyes widened. "You wouldn't. The door was unlocked."

"Try me. Anyway, just because it was unlocked doesn't mean you should be coming in here uninvited."

Sighing, she handed over the phone to him. "I could give you a tip about the Vojnik," she smiled seductively.

"I'm listening," he muttered as he ran back through the pictures that she had taken.

Putting her hand on her hip, she stuck it out and focused on him. When she noticed that his eyes were on her, she pushed her chest out slightly. "I heard they're planning to intercept your drug shipment next week."

He laughed. "You're cute, but if you wanna seduce me, you're gonna have to do a little more than stick your tits out. About the other thing, which shipment?"

That pissed her off. She *was* cute. People told her she was cute all the time, yet he acted like she was begging him to throw her on the ground and take her. His question confused her as well. "There's more than one shipment?

How many of these do you guys do every week?" she asked, her brain working overtime.

He shrugged, the leather he wore over his shoulders creaking with the movement. "I dunno, Ms. Rager. You tell me. How many are there in any given week?"

It was then she realized he was playing her. Taking the information she was giving but not giving her anything in return. Heat reddened her cheeks, and she held her hand out for her phone.

"You got what you wanted, give me my phone back."

He pressed a few buttons and smiled at her before placing it back in the palm of her hand. "I like you, so I'm gonna be nice. You're stickin' your nose into things you don't understand here. Your curiosity is goin' to get someone killed. Do you want someone's blood on your hands? Because it's goin' to be there if you don't back off. Don't make me warn you again. Next time I won't be so nice."

Turning her around by the shoulders, he pushed her out of the front door and locked it as she stumbled out onto the front porch. He knew without a doubt that she would be back, but he hoped that next time she was a little bit smarter.

Fuming, Meredith made her way back down to her duplex.

"Ugh. That man."

Grabbing her phone out of her pocket, she tried to make a phone call only for it to tell her that her passcode was incorrect. Again she tried, knowing that she had input the correct one. Realization dawned after the fourth try. Seething, she marched back over to the house and beat on the door until it opened.

"Can I help you?" he asked, laughing as he saw the look on her face.

"Change it back."

"I'm not sure I know what you mean?"

"You, Tyler Blackfoot, are a bastard. Change my damn passcode back. You've put me in my place, and I get it."

He grabbed the phone from her hand and did as she asked. "Games aren't that fun to play are they? Remember that when dealing with the club, Ms. Rager."

"Damnit." Liam shouted as he threw his phone down on the bed that they had just made up with fresh sheets for Mandy at his house.

"What?" Denise asked, looking up at him in alarm.

His heart ached as he looked at her. It had been a long twenty-four hours, and it showed on her face. A large bruise marred her cheekbone, her nose was still red and swollen, her eyes had blackened, and you could still see bits of dried blood on her scalp.

"Club business," he answered, his voice clipped.

"Is that all I'm allowed to know?" she asked, folding her arms over her chest. She wasn't sure how well this would work for her. Being by yourself meant you were never kept in the dark – having someone else calling the shots would take some getting used to.

"That's all you get to know. I gotta go, but I'll be back in a little while. Make yourselves at home. There's plenty of food."

As he reached the bedroom door, he turned abruptly and came back to stand in front of her. Looking up at him, she was afraid to move. Tenderly, he cupped her cheek with the palm of his hand and swept his large thumb over the bruise that had appeared.

"Get some sleep. Things will look way different when you wake up. Roni will make sure that the kids are taken care of. Just rest," he whispered. More than anything, he wanted to comfort her. To explain that *this* wasn't how things always went. Maybe lean in and give her a gentle kiss on the lips, show her another side of himself, but he knew this wasn't the time.

The moment was too intimate for her, too soon after everything that had happened. She stepped out of his personal space and shook her head slightly as if to clear it.

"I can't, I have to work tonight."

His eyes hardened. "Not anymore. I'm gonna take care of you for a while. Roni already called and told them you quit."

She flushed angrily. She had never even had to consult with anyone about her decisions before, and now others were making decisions for her that she didn't even agree with.

"Think about what you say before you speak," he warned her.

Was it really worth it to go to war with him? She questioned. Deciding she was just too tired to put up a fight, she answered. "Just go do what you have to. I'll be here when you get back, hopefully with a few hours sleep under my belt. Maybe then we can talk about this like mature adults."

He nodded in agreement. Before leaving, he gave into his desire. He leaned down and brushed a soft kiss against the bruise on her cheek. "I really am sorry that happened. I should have stopped it before it started."

"I know." And she really did. "Go do what you have to do."

She walked him to the front door of the house. Her eyes followed him as he got on his bike and started it up. As he revved the engine, he looked back at her and raised his hand in a wave. Denise could see the smirk on his face and her heart sped up just a little bit.

This was dangerous in so many ways. She was in so deep, she didn't even know if there would ever be a way out, didn't know now if she even wanted a way out. That's what scared her the most. How quickly she seemed to have accepted this. Only the future would tell her if she had made the right decision or not.

Chapter Nine

"**A**nybody know what this is about?" Tyler asked, putting his arms out and laying his head on them. It had been a long couple of nights for everyone.

The officers sat around the main table in the clubhouse, waiting to see what they had all been summoned back for.

Liam shook his head, answering Tyler's yawn with one of his own. "There's no telling." He sat up a little straighter, stretching to keep himself awake.

The group looked up as they heard another person come through the door. William Walker strutted down the aisle, gazing at each of them before taking the seat at the head of the table. With the power of a president, he watched the group of men that had assembled, daring them to speak before he did. When it became evident they wouldn't, he started talking with the booming voice he used when he knew he had a great idea.

"Tomorrow night, the Vojnik are supposed to intercept our drug shipment. We're going to let them."

Mummers went up around the table as they all started to protest.

"That shipment is one of two going out, and the boxes all have tracking devices inside the cardboard. We're gonna let them get it and watch where they take it. Then we're gonna let them know that the reporter squealed like a pig."

Tyler winced. He knew the Vojnik, and they would not appreciate that she had shared information. His conscience prickled a little, but he couldn't let that show. That was a weakness he didn't want William to know about right now. "Good, she's been a pain in our ass for months." That should keep William from knowing what he was thinking.

William nodded. "This way we kill two birds with one stone. Maybe we can get her off our asses for a while and figure out where they're headquartering out of. Since their clubhouse got raided a few months ago, we have absolutely no idea what they're doing."

After hashing out a plan, the group broke up, each going their separate ways. Liam walked with Tyler to their bikes.

"I saw your face in there, brother. Does it bother you we're taking the reporter's tip?" Liam asked, covering another yawn with the back of his hand.

"It's not that really," Tyler answered, rolling his head on his shoulders. "I just have a bad feelin' about it."

It was a well-known fact in the club that when Tyler had a feeling, they better watch themselves. Everyone believed it had to do with his Native American heritage.

"For us or her?"

"Not sure. I can't seem to get a bead on it. We'll get a lot of information out of this, but we'll also put a target on our backs. I'm not sure knowing where the Vojnik are headquartered will be worth the risk. I mean, yeah, we'll be able to keep an eye on them and possibly stop their part of the drug trade, but at what cost? That's something your father doesn't seem to weigh very well," Tyler grinned.

That was the truth. As a leader William Walker had one glaring weakness, he never weighed the end result with the risk. It sometimes led to bloodshed and turf wars. At the very least, the consequences of this raid would be almost instant. They were potentially messing with the livelihood of another club. There would be retaliation.

"Are you gonna warn her?"

"I feel like I should. At this point we've got our hands full with the Vojnik. Trying to figure out where they're going with their operation and what they've got going on. I don't want to have to worry about her too, but I feel like the target we put on our back will be just as much on hers too."

Liam nodded. "You know what this feels like to me? A setup. It may not be, but it just feels too convenient. They tell her, and she tells us."

Those thoughts were what would make Liam a good leader when the time came. He wouldn't dare question William, but they very well could have just put themselves in a bad situation.

"Maybe it's not really a setup for us, maybe it's a setup for her," Tyler theorized.

'Good point. Either way, I'm gonna go get some sleep. We have a lot to get accomplished tomorrow. We need to be fresh for it. I gotta put some time in at the shop too, we're behind. As usual."

The two clapped hands and half hugged before parting ways and getting on their own bikes.

Denise sat in the kitchen of Liam's home nursing a cup of decaf coffee. She contemplated the events of the last few days as she swirled the black liquid around. It had been a whirlwind to say the least. Out of all the ways the events could have played out, this was the most surprising ending of them all. She had never expected to move in with Liam Walker.

Getting up, she began walking around the home that she would be calling her own for the foreseeable future. It was funny, she'd had definite ideas when she had thought of how and where Liam lived. The picture in her head had been vastly different from what greeted her now. In her mind she had imagined a run-down trailer with a state of the art garage for his bike located within shouting distance of the clubhouse.

Reality was much different. A two-story house sat on a hill about two miles from the clubhouse. The driveway and landscaping looked like something she would have done to her own home. A large porch wrapped all the way around the house with the back section screened-in. She marveled at the work that had been done there. It had full electricity, ceiling fans, a couch, a table, and a chaise over to the side. She could foresee many afternoons and nights of reading out there if given the chance.

The inside of the house was a huge surprise as well. It didn't look like a bachelor lived in the space at all. It was warm with the feelings of hearth and home. Pictures of family members were up everywhere as well some that she recognized as members of the club. The walls were all painted neutral tones and everything seemed to match. The bathrooms had large showers and bathtubs. The two rooms that her kids occupied in were good sized and looked like they had been specifically built for children.

It was interesting to her that this seemed to be a home built for a family.

Denise heard the low hum of a motorcycle coming up the driveway. Feeling uncomfortable in her new surroundings, she got up and went to the window, wanting to make sure it was Liam.

She watched, covered by the darkness of the room he had indicated was hers, as he parked and took off the helmet he wore. His shoulder length dark hair was disheveled, and her fingers itched to run through it. As if he felt her eyes on him, he glanced up to the second story window where she stood. It was so dark, she was sure he didn't see her, but just in case she dropped the curtain and scampered away from the window.

This whole turn of events confused her. Four days ago she had been broke and facing foreclosure on her home. Today she was in an entirely new home and had money from delivering drugs for an outlaw motorcycle club. For the first time since she had lost her factory job, she had some breathing room. She didn't have the weight on her shoulders of having to feed her family and put gas in her car. It was freeing, liberating. Not to mention after making those checks out to the credit card companies, she knew she would no longer be getting calls that hounded her at all hours of the night.

For the first time in years, she felt like she could be something other than a mother, she could be a woman. Maybe she could explore some of the feelings she'd let hibernate for so long. As soon as those thoughts crossed her mind, she immediately felt guilty. What about her children? Shouldn't she want to do better for them? Instead of worrying about them, she was worrying about how she could be a woman again. On the other hand, one day those children would leave and then she would again be stuck on her own. There had to be a middle ground, and she meant to find it. The man was just too gorgeous not to look at.

"I mean, really Denise, you're in a home with a man who could be a supermodel," she whispered to herself. "If you can't figure out what to do with him on your own then you need to join the nunnery."

Knuckles rapped lightly at her bedroom door, and she thought about pretending to be asleep for a moment before her subconscious kicked her own ass.

"Yeah," she questioned softly.

The door opened and she wanted to lick her lips. He'd obviously taken a shower in the time she'd spent contemplating, and her body took notice. He wore dark sweatpants and a white tank top covered his chest. Hair, curly now that it was wet, clung to the sides of his neck, dripping lightly onto his bare shoulders.

"I just wanted to make sure you're comfortable," he whispered, walking further into the room. "Did you find everything you need?"

She nodded and then realized that he couldn't see her in the dark. Stretching up, she turned the bedside lamp on, blinking as light flooded the room.

"I did," she stared at him.

Clearing his throat, he sat next to her on the bed. "I was pretty rude earlier, and I didn't mean to be. I told you to treat this place like home and I meant it. If you need something that I don't have here, we'll get it."

"I know. It's a gorgeous home," she complimented.

A grin transformed his face. "Besides my bikes it's my pride and joy. I'm glad you're comfortable here."

"I am."

He ran his hands along his fleece covered thighs before standing up. "Well I'll let you get to sleep, it's going to be a long day tomorrow. Hell, it's been a long day *today*."

"What happens tomorrow?" After the events of this night, she wasn't sure she wanted to actually get to tomorrow.

"You'll be told what you need to know, but it won't be much. Just trust me in what I tell you and what others tell you to do." He knew it was a lot for her to take on his word, but it was all he had. "Get some sleep."

With that, he was gone, leaving her to contemplate just what he had told her. Everything was such a secret in this life. It would take some getting used to. But if that's what would need to happen to keep her kids and herself safe, she would do whatever she had to do.

Chapter Ten

A drenaline coursed through Tyler as he took the Kentucky roads he loved at much higher speeds than was legal. This was *it*, why he loved to ride his bike. The feeling of the wind against his face, the sound of it rushing by his ears and running through his hair. The freedom of no one telling him where to go or what to do. Listening to common sense, he slowed down to take the turn that would lead him to Denise's neighborhood. The club had just successfully let the Vojnik steal their drug shipment. It had gone off without a hitch. It was time to let Meredith know what had taken place.

As he approached her duplex, he became breathless. The woman really was beautiful, but she was everything he'd always said he never wanted. Pulling into her driveway, he shut off his bike and swaggered up to the front door. Her car was in the drive, so he knew she was home. Before he could knock, she threw the door open.

"What the fuck is the matter with you?" she hissed, grabbing his cut and hauling him inside.

"Hey." he yelled sharply. "You don't touch that."

Quickly she dropped her hands. "Sorry, but again what the fuck is the matter with you? How dare you park in my driveway and walk up like you own the damn place?"

Irritated, he scowled. "Look Princess, I came by to let you know that we did a job on the Vojnik tonight. Since you're the one who squealed on them like a damn pig, I figured I'd warn you. What you do with that warning is up to you, but I thought you should know."

She opened her mouth to speak and then shut it abruptly. Had he actually just done something nice for her?

"Are you expecting a thank you or something?" she asked, folding her arms over her chest.

"You know what? Forget it. I have a feeling they leaked that information to you to see if you'd tell us, and guess what....you did. When they realize that, you're gonna be in a lot more trouble than you know what do with. Take the information and do with it what you will, but don't come crying to me when this all backfires."

He turned and walked out without another word. For the first time since she'd started these investigations, she felt uneasy. Was that really what the Vojnik had planned? Had she really just put herself in a hole she'd never be able to dig herself out of?

"Motherfucker." Liam muttered as he spotted the blue lights behind him.

Wanting to do anything to avoid jail time at this point, he politely pulled over and dug his license and registration out of his saddlebags. As the sheriff came around the side of the bike, he spotted the face in his side view mirror and grinned. This was an old friend, but he could just as easily be an enemy.

"Rooster, how ya doin'?" he asked, grinning up at the redheaded sheriff's deputy.

"Not too bad," he answered. It didn't escape Liam's notice that he casually rested his hand on the butt of his gun.

"By the way you're standin' I'll take it this ain't a social call."

"You would be correct in that assumption and don't be callin' me Rooster. You of all people know my name is Officer Hancock. We had some reports of loud motorcycles and shots fired out near the old Garvin Lane Bridge. You know anything about that?"

"Can't say that I do. Can you place me or my boys there?"

Officer Hancock smirked. "C'mon Walker, we're old friends."

"That's right *Rooster*, we are. We ran these roads when we were teenagers, but we're not on the same side now are we?"

"Your choice. You could have come my way, and we both know it, "Rooster accused, looking down at his one-time friend.

"Are you stoppin' me for somethin', or are you just gettin' your rocks off by harrassin' me?"

Handing the license and registration back to Liam, Rooster put his sunglasses on and looked down at him again. "Don't let me find out this was your bunch. You know it won't take much for you to go back to jail."

"Officer Hancock, is that a threat?"

"Nope, William Walker Jr., that's a promise. Friendship doesn't go above the law."

"Neither does common courtesy. You remember that, and we'll be good."

He sped off, throwing gravel at the cop car still parked behind him, daring Hancock to flip the lights on and pull him over again. Instead, he sounded the siren once in warning and headed in the opposite direction.

Pulling up to the clubhouse, Liam was surprised to see a couple of the other brothers already there. They had just pulled the Vojnik job and had separated to get the hell out of dodge. The run-in with Rooster must have taken longer than he thought. Parking his bike, he got off and walked in. A large group sat around the laptop computer that Travis Steele had set on one of the tables. They were watching the GPS trackers from the drug shipment.

"What's this?" he asked, having a seat as he allowed his eyes to adjust to the darkness of the indoors.

Steele grinned as he looked at his VP. "This is technology at its finest. We're getting a motherfucking roadmap to where the Vojnik clubhouse is now located. Hopefully, this is where they keep their technology too. What my geeky little fingers would do if I could get my hands on some of the stuff they're bringing in from Europe."

"Looks like they're takin' it to Barren County. Wonder why they're taking it so far up the parkway?" one of the men asked.

"Probably because they don't want to keep it around us. Let's face it, none of us would have thought Barren County when we started this. They've been smart."

Liam watched as the tracking device did its thing. He was familiar with that area, and he was pretty sure they were going to an old warehouse that used to be an automotive plant before the downturn in the economy. Heaven Hill had done some protection in that area for a local loan shark, and if memory served him correctly, it was a large facility.

"We need to get on the Property Assessor's site and see who that property lists too," Liam said, taking down the approximate location of the dot on the map.

"Do you think they'd be stupid enough to list it to themselves?" Steele asked.

"I don't know, but we want to make sure if we blow it to hell we're not destroying a profitable piece of property for a friend. What if they're renting it? If the city owns it, we'd be in some deep shit too."

Steele nodded and pulled up the Property Assessor's website for the adjacent county. It only took a few moments to find it was listed to an LLC.

"Is it a front you think?" Steele asked, rubbing his chin.

"Not sure. I think we need to do a little more research on it. Maybe get one of the women to go visit the courthouse and see what we can find out. We need to be smart about this. Tyler had a feelin' last night. We need to be talkin' to the old man about it too. Shouldn't he be here soon?"

The group began to look uncomfortable. "Where is he?"

Nobody said anything, nobody met his eyes and one brother even started whistling. "Where is he?"

"I think he went to see your mom," someone mumbled.

That was all it took to put him in a murderous mood. In a matter of moments he was out the door and on his bike.

"Did you have to tell him?" Steele asked, his blue eyes glaring at the brother who had opened his mouth.

"He asked, I answered."

"Don't do it again."

"How are you getting along?" Roni asked.

She and Denise sat inside the screened-in porch, enjoying the beauty of the afternoon. The kids were upstairs doing homework and playing on the laptops that had been mysteriously provided for them. Denise wasn't sure if it had been Roni or Liam, but she was grateful.

"Not too bad, I'm just not sure what my place is here, ya know? I feel like I'm invading his territory, but he keeps telling me to treat this house like home."

"Trust me, if he didn't want you here, you wouldn't be here. He must see something in you and your kids."

Denise shrugged. "I dunno, we haven't really talked that much. He hasn't really been around."

"Yeah, word has it there was a job today. Of course I don't know any details, but last I heard everyone was safe."

A feeling of dread settled over her. "Do people sometimes *not* come back safe?

"Honestly? Depends on what they're doing. This life isn't for everyone. There have been casualties and even fatalities of our wars. It's just a fact of this life."

That was what scared Denise. What if her kids were caught in the crossfire?

"I don't mean to scare you, don't get me wrong. Ninety percent of the time things are fine, but there are turf wars and pissed off clubs. There can be dangerous times."

As she opened her mouth to respond, she heard Liam's motorcycle coming up the drive. "Guess he's back."

Roni listened intently. "He's pissed though."

A look of disbelief crossed her face. "How can you tell that by the roar of his bike?"

"Lots of practice. You'll be able to do it sooner or later."

He came barreling through the front door and stomped all the way through the house and out onto the porch where they sat.

"What crawled up your ass?" Roni questioned her brother. "We were having a nice, quiet time." It amazed Denise that anyone spoke to him in that way.

"Dad's gone to see Lauren."

Just like that, the mood shifted for Roni too.

"Who's Lauren?" Denise questioned softly.

Liam glared at her before turning around and stomping out again.

"Forgive him, he doesn't deal well when she's mentioned. Lauren's our mother. She abandoned us. For some reason, our father still loves her. Give Liam some time, he'll come around. He's just gotta get over it. C'mon girl. Talk me out of this bad mood."

Smiling, Denise started rambling, enjoying her afternoon acting like any other woman in the world. She did, however, put the little tidbit of information about Liam's background in the back of her mind. When the time was right, she would ask her questions and hopefully get her answers.

Chapter Eleven

William rolled over taking Lauren's body with his. It wasn't very often that they did this, but sometimes they just got caught up in the memories and the moment.

Even after what they had just shared, her stomach bunched with nerves. She had to say what was on her mind, but she knew it would not be received well. "You've got to watch it with Liam," she started carefully.

He groaned. He didn't want to hear this. He hated when she acted like she knew her son. The only way to get her to stop was to throw hurtful words back in her face.

"Shut the fuck up," he told her. "You don't know anything about your son, and you especially don't know anything about our relationship. You're the one that left."

Tears sprang to her eyes and she turned away, hiding her face so that he couldn't see. That was the one thing she hated. He always brought up what a bad mother she was. They could never stay on good terms for more than a few hours, and usually those hours were spent between the sheets. It didn't help that ultimately she knew the words he spoke were true. She was a mother of the worst kind, not even able to be called *Mom*.

"Because you won't let me know about your relationship," she whispered, letting warm tears trail down her cheeks.

The bed dipped as he got up, and she could hear him put his clothes back on. His anger was obvious in the sound of the fabric slapping as he covered his body.

"I gotta be gettin' back to the clubhouse. Do you need any money?"

Add that to the list of things she positively hated. He got what he wanted, and then he had the nerve to ask if she needed money. Like she was his whore, like she didn't still wear his ring on her finger. Like in the eyes of the law and God they weren't still married. She may have given up on their children, but she hadn't given up on him. "Keep your damn money. I don't need it."

Paper money fluttered as it hit her shoulder and she flinched. Refusing to turn over, she heard the door slam on his way out.

"Lauren, when are you going to stop doing this to yourself?" she whispered as she rolled over and grabbed the money that sat on the bed.

She counted $400 – enough to pay almost all of her rent. It never failed to strike her as shitty that both Liam and William owned their own homes, even Roni had been left out of that. They each had motorcycles and cars, it didn't look they wanted for anything. While she struggled. Both financially and emotionally. The little apartment she rented was hot in the summer and cold in the winter. The pipes froze at least once a year, and the shower never seemed to have hot water. Her thirteen-year-old car was on its last legs, and her bank account could use a few thousand dollars so that she could get a little spontaneous with her spending. She sighed deeply, brushing the moisture from her face. This was not how she had ever though her life would turn out, even in her wildest dreams.

"Mrs. Walker, it looks like you've got yourself a healthy baby boy."

Her heart sank in what should have been one of the happiest moments of her life. In a flash, she saw this little boy's future, and she was scared. For herself, her husband, her older daughter, and this innocent little boy who had no idea that his future had just been sealed.

William and his friends had started a motorcycle club that was quickly turning into something very illegal. When she had become pregnant, she had prayed every night that it would once again be a little girl. This boy would be heir apparent to those illegal activities and that motorcycle club. There was nothing about this that she liked.

"Thanks for giving me a son, Lauren. The next generation is well on its way."

His eyes shone brightly with pride as he held the tiny bundle of joy in his arms. Any love that he felt for the child she had just birthed was replaced with greed for more power and the guarantee of the line of succession for Heaven Hill. She realized at that moment that she would have to leave. Her throat tightened as she fought to hold back the fear that she already felt. She would take whatever time she had with this son of hers, and it would have to last her the rest of her life. She knew that as surely as she knew the sun would rise in the east and set in the west.

Shaking her head, Lauren got out of the bed and went to the bathroom. Reaching into the shower, she turned it on and waited for it to warm – as much as it ever did. While she waited, her mind worked overtime.

"He will not be a member of this gang." Lauren screamed, pressing her finger into his chest. Fear tightened her throat and tears streamed down her face.

William had the audacity to smile. "We're motorcycle enthusiasts."

"You are criminals – getting worse by the day," she accused. *"I don't want to be a part of this anymore."* It had gradually been getting more and more illegal, the stakes getting higher and the risk becoming more deadly. She wanted to take her kids and run as far and as fast as she could, but she knew it would never be far enough that he couldn't find her.

He grabbed her around the wrist and hauled her so close their noses touched. His grip tightened until she groaned aloud and more tears spilled from her eyes. "You leave this club, and you leave alone. The kids stay with me, and that's final. You're not taking them."

She sobbed. "You can't keep me from my kids." The worst feeling was that she knew he could and would take them from her. There was absolutely nothing he wouldn't do to prove his authority over her. The secret she kept so closely hidden wouldn't even help her.

"And you can't keep me from mine. You need to make a decision here, wife of mine."

Lauren had never been so conflicted in her life. She couldn't stand by and watch this man ruin her son, the one that was so kind hearted and climbed into her lap every night asking for a bed time story. He was the most precocious five-year-old she had ever seen.

At the same time, she felt like she couldn't leave, and if she tried she would be dead.

Lauren remembered those days so clearly. At five years old she had known that he would be such a good man. The glimpses she'd seen of him throughout the years had shown her that despite all the heartache, he had grown into an amazing man. No thanks to her.

"Mommy, look at what I did today."

Lauren looked up from where she stood cooking hamburgers for their dinner to see William and the kids returning from the store. "What did you do?" she grinned at the little boy who had stolen her heart.

"Got a candy bar."

"How did you do that? I didn't send any money with you." Immediately her stomach dropped. She knew what this was, and it was the beginning that would never have an end.

His eyes sparkled, much like his father. "I stole it, and nobody caught me. Dad said I earned my keep."

"You did what?" she asked, her voice calm. She was trying to keep it together – to not scream at a little boy who just wanted to make his dad proud.

"I stoled it."

He was so proud and William had such a hold over him, she knew in that moment she had to leave. She couldn't stand by and watch this little boy turn into the man that his father had become. Her heart couldn't take it.

The water finally warm, she adjusted it to a temperature that she could stand. Stepping in, she let it flow over her, allowing it to wash the sadness away from her body. The pain of missing her family had recently manifested itself as a physical ache, and she hoped to one day wash *that* pain away. Taking a deep breath, she exhaled and focused on the small tasks at hand. That was the way she had lived the last twenty-seven years, putting one foot in front of the other and focusing on small tasks. At least then she felt like she had accomplished something with her life instead of failing as a mother.

She hoped and prayed that one day she would be able to make Liam understand the reasons for what she had done. That all the pain and suffering they both had gone through had been the only solution she had seen at the time to an unforgiving problem. To a man she had been deathly afraid of. She had been witness to things that she hoped one day to forget. If she was ever lucky enough to get that second chance, she would make sure it counted and that William Walker would never have a hold over her again.

Chapter Twelve

"**T**he club needs your help."

Denise winced as she heard Liam's deep voice speak those words. The last time someone had said them to her, she had ended up having to move out of her home and having an argument with her only friend. She put aside the book she was reading and looked up at him. "With what?"

Liam gifted her with a heart-stopping smile that caused her breath to catch. She was sure in the past that smile had gotten him into the panties of many women. "Oh you're good," she laughed. "Really, what do you want?" She turned so that she gave him her full attention.

"The Vojnik are occupying a warehouse in Glasgow. It's owned by an LLC. We need to figure out who spearheads this LLC. It could be the Vojnik, or it could be someone on our side. We need you to go to the courthouse and do a little investigating. Dress like you should be there, we can even make you a badge that says you work there. I need any information you can get me," he explained, his intense gaze boring into hers. She got the feeling this was important.

Motioning to the sweatpants and t-shirt she wore, she curled up her nose. "Am I doin' this today? Because if I am, I have no clothes that make me look like I work in a courthouse. In fact, I have none that make me look like I work anywhere."

He held up a finger, and she watched as he made his way back into the house.

"So much for spending a day relaxing on the screened-in porch, reading a romance novel," she mumbled, following him inside.

He came out of a vacant bedroom and held a wad of cash out to her. "Go get what you need."

Her mouth gaped as he put the money in her hand. Just how much money was lying around this house? "How much is here?" Who had money hidden in their house like this? It was a reminder of the kind of people she was spending time with.

"Enough to get you what you need. Don't hesitate to get anything else you want." He was careful to break that sentence up into needs and wants. He was pretty sure she hadn't purchased a want in a very long time – most everything had probably been necessities.

This didn't sit well with her. She had never been taken care of in her life and she sure didn't want to start now. "This is a loan," she told him, those words making her feel at least a little bit better about the situation.

"No, it's not. I'm asking you to do a job for me, and I am providing you with the tools that you need in order to complete that job. I'm doing nothing that a normal manager wouldn't do for their employee."

She rolled her eyes. "Give me a fucking break. You know that this isn't a normal situation. Just let me go get what I need to."

Liam laughed when he saw heat color her cheeks. He liked that little bit of backbone she showed to him. He loved when she got sassy. Grabbing her purse, she started to leave.

"Hang on," he placed his hand on her shoulder, exerting slight pressure.

"What now?" she asked, putting her hands on her hips and tapping her foot.

"Take my truck," he handed her a set of keys.

"Where is it?"

"Main garage, it's the gunmetal gray, Harley Davidson Edition."

"Of course."

Placing the keys in her hand, he continued to hold on to them until her eyes met his. "Keep safe, and whatever you do, don't scratch it. If you do that I'll expect you to fix it." A shit-eating grin tilted the corners of his mouth and he raised his eyebrows in suggestion. "But you could pay me back using carnal means."

Her breathing picked up slightly. No man, ever, had blatantly flirted with her before. It was as much arousing as it was exciting. She wracked her brain for an appropriate comeback.

"You wish," she threw back at him before leaving the house quickly. That was a good comeback right? She tried to convince herself that it was as she made her way to his truck.

"How do women do this?" Denise mumbled as she stared blankly at racks and racks of clothes. There were a multitude of styles and colors, but nothing that she thought would look good on her. She didn't even know where to start. The measly amount of clothing she'd bought in her lifetime had never prepared her for this. Not even her 'shopping spree' from the other day.

She needed help. Pulling out her cell phone, she dialed Roni's number and waited impatiently for her to pick up. "Roni? Hey, I need clothing help."

In minutes she'd explained the situation and was waiting for her friend to show up and guide her. Roni had guaranteed that she had a friend who would know exactly what to get.

"Denise." She spun around, watching as Roni and her friend made their way into the store. The woman at her side was tall, curvy, and built in the fashion that men called stacked. Looking at this other woman made Denise want to run home in despair.

"Hey," Roni greeted. "I called Liam to see what he had you doing. That way Sparkles would know what to get for you."

"Sparkles?" Denise laughed. "What is she a stripper?"

"Sure am, honey. I work down at Wet Wanda's."

Feeling embarrassed, Denise started to apologize. "I'm so sorry, I was just kidding. I didn't mean to offend you. Sometimes my mouth gets the better of me."

"Oh, you didn't. I've been a stripper for a long time. I make a good livin' strippin' at the club. They give good tips, you should come on down sometime. I guarantee you, once I'm done you could set the place on fire."

Denise blushed. No one had ever spoken to her like this. There was no way this woman could convince anyone that she had a stripper's body. She and Roni looked at one another, not sure what to say.

Breaking the silence, Sparkles smiled. "Okay ladies, let's get Denise into some sexy office wear. I promise you, by the time I'm done, Liam Walker will be drooling at your feet and he'll never ask you to work for the club again." She clapped her hands together and called over a sales girl.

Two hours later, Denise looked like she belonged in a courthouse, and her head was spinning. She could even admit that she did look a little bit like she was ready to star in a porno. The skirt was just short enough, the button down shirt just tight enough. Sparkles was a force to be reckoned with. Without realizing it, she had new clothes, new makeup, and a new hairdo.

"I don't really think this was what Liam meant when he told me to look like I work in a courthouse. I don't think he meant new hair and new makeup."

Sparkles grinned. "I'm sure he'll like what we've done with you."

The way Sparkles talked about Liam, it made her wonder if they had been an item before. Denise wanted to ask, but she knew without a doubt that she would be jealous and she couldn't deal with that right now.

The three of them left the mall and headed to their vehicles. As Denise went to get into the truck, Roni whistled and Sparkles eyes bugged.

"He let you drive his truck?"

"No he didn't *let* me. He *told* me to drive it. I was kind of against the whole thing."

"You are in way over your head with my brother, Denise Cunningham."

"I had that feeling myself," Denise sighed. "I don't want to be this far over my head."

"With him," Roni said placing a hand on her friend's back, "you don't realize you're that deep until you're neck deep with no place to go. Enjoy it while it lasts."

And that was the bitch of the situation. Denise knew that it wouldn't last. The only thing she could do was take control of it with both hands and dare him to make her let go.

Denise pulled up outside of the Barren County Courthouse and put the truck in park before shutting it off. Roni had provided her with a badge that claimed she was an assistant to the County Property Assessor. It would give her access to the property records that she needed. Before walking in, she took a deep breath and straightened her shoulders. She had to look like she belonged, she had to own this.

Her heels clicked on the floor as she made her way through the building. It was a bit disconcerting to hear just how loud they were. So much for being inconspicuous. She slowed down as she reached a row of offices and scoped out which one she needed. As she entered, a harried older woman ran up to her.

"Thank God you're here! The temp agency sent you right?" she asked, eyeing the badge Denise wore. "You're my new assistant."

"Yes ma'am. I'm Cindy Thompson," she introduced herself with the fake name they'd given her. "Just point me in the direction of what you need me to do, and I'll just go ahead and get to work."

Within minutes, Denise sat at a computer that had everything she needed at her fingertips. Quickly, she pulled the piece of paper with the address of the building out of her purse and logged into the county records. It was at that moment she realized how thankful she was that they hadn't used her real name. This was an illegal activity – something she found herself doing a lot for Liam recently.

Locating the property record that she needed, she clicked into it and scrolled down to the property transfers section. Her eyebrows furrowed as she saw that the property had been quit claimed three months before from a Richard Joyce to a PlayMakers LLC. Thinking like she imagined a criminal would think, she did a search for other records under both of those names. There were numerous properties that had been quit claimed exactly the same way. Pulling a USB drive out of her purse, she copied all the information that she figured they would need and placed it in her purse before standing up.

"Excuse me, can you point me in the direction of the ladies room?"

The woman who'd met her when she'd first come in looked at her suspiciously, noting the purse at her side.

"Time of the month," she whispered loudly, giggling a little to cover up her nervousness.

"Sure thing, it's down the hall to the left."

As quick as she could, Denise made it down the hall and out the door. Her heart beat wildly as she all but ran for the truck. Not bothering to look back, she started it up and drove away. Hopefully she had what the club needed.

Chapter Thirteen

"Liam, you got a call."

Rolling out from underneath the car he was working on, Liam sat up quickly. His first thought was Denise needed help. Grabbing his cell phone, he saw he hadn't missed any calls from her, but that didn't mean that everything was okay. It surprised him that his hands shook as he picked up the shop phone.

"Yeah," he answered gruffly, fear making him sound more harsh than he had intended to.

"Liam?" the small voice that asked for him sounded thick with tears and heavy with fear.

He wracked his brain trying to figure out who it was. The person knew him well enough to call him at work. "Mandy? Is that you?"

She sniffed, and he could almost see the nod he was sure she gave. "Yeah."

Being in a motorcycle gang, he'd not had much experience with kids at all, much less teenage girls. He waited a beat for her to tell him what she wanted. But when he realized it wasn't coming, he tried to soften his voice as he asked, "Honey, what do you need?"

Tears started in earnest, and she blabbed a mouthful of words – none of which he could make out except for the name Drew. He heard shuffling on the other end and then another female voice.

"Sir? My name is Stacey Young, and I'm the secretary at Warren County Middle School. Sorry to bother you."

"That's alright," he answered, confused as to why they had called him.

"We tried to reach Denise, but her phone went straight to voice mail. When they had a change of address here at the school, you were added to their emergency contact information."

He hadn't been informed of that, but he could understand why she had added him. He also figured she had turned off her cell phone while she was doing the job for the club. "Okay, and what can I help you with?"

"There's been an issue with Andrew today. He and another boy got into a fight, and we need someone to come get him. He's been sent home for the rest of the day and will possibly be expelled," she explained matter-of-factly.

It was on the tip of his tongue to ask what Mandy had to do with this, but he figured he would save time and just ask questions when he got there. "I work a few miles from there. I'll be there soon."

Cursing, he slammed the phone down and looked at Tyler, who gazed at him, eyebrows raised. "I gotta go, Drew got into a fight at school."

Tyler laughed. "Good luck on this one, Daddy."

Liam felt his breath hitch. That's exactly what this felt like, he was going to pick his son up at school after getting into a fight. He wondered if he should punish the boy, but he felt so inept that he didn't know how he was supposed to handle this situation.

"Yeah, thanks. I think I'm just gonna have to wing it. If Denise calls, can you tell her where I am? They called her, but she didn't answer."

"Will do. I'll cover for you with the old man too."

Tyler was the type of friend that everyone should have. "Thanks man. See ya later."

"So what you're saying is he's in trouble for stickin' up for his sister?"

Liam was getting more pissed by the minute, but he was trying hard not to show it. He'd even left his cut in Tyler's truck, which he'd had to borrow when he realized he'd let Denise take his.

"What I'm saying, Mr. Walker, is that we can't stand for fighting of any kind within the school, and, regardless of how well meaning it was, he will need to be punished. He's being suspended for three days."

Glancing over at Drew, Liam took in the dried blood on his mouth and nose, the torn shirt and the torn jeans. He'd seen the other boy as he had walked in and Drew had definitely given as good as he had gotten.

"Mr. Tucker, I'll sign off on it as long as you assure me that the other boy is punished not only for the fighting but also for the lewd comment he made to Mandy."

"Now, we all know that boys will be boys," Mr. Tucker stuttered.

"Boys do not tell young girls that their 'tits are hot' and then ask young girls if they 'give head'. I think we can all agree on that." Liam fought to keep his voice even and calm when he wanted to rip the kid from limb to limb. "The fact of the matter is, that should be reported, and I'm assuming you aren't going to do that because this other child's father is on the school board. So let's just make a gentlemen's agreement that you will suspend that little shit for six days, and if he ever comes near her again *I'll* take care of it. Forget letting *her brother* beat his ass."

Mr. Tucker had the presence of mind to realize that Liam wasn't kidding. "I think we can agree on that."

"Fine, let me sign his paperwork and get Mandy, and we'll be out of here."

"She doesn't have to go home," Mr. Tucker argued.

"I'm not making her sit here today after what she's been through. She's a sensitive kid."

Within minutes Liam had signed all the paperwork and signed the kids out, and they were headed down Louisville Road. Both of them were quiet as they sat next to him.

"I'm not mad at you two."

"Mom's gonna be," Mandy whispered, tears already in her eyes.

"For what?" Liam asked, not understanding.

"She always tells us to walk away," Drew answered. "To not rise to anyone's teasing."

Liam could see where she was coming from, but he happened to agree with Drew on this. He wouldn't let anyone talk about Roni like they had talked about Mandy.

"For what it's worth, dude, I would have done the same thing had some fuckwad messed with Roni like that. Shit, sorry. I shouldn't cuss."

Mandy giggled, covering her mouth. She was an innocence that he hadn't had in his life – ever. So untainted by the outside world.

Drew was the complete opposite. He *knew* reality and just accepted it – probably to shield Mandy from it.

"We won't tell," she assured him.

"Are you alright?" he turned his attention to her brother.

"My nose and mouth hurt, but I'm okay," he shrugged. "My hand actually hurts worse than anything."

Liam glanced down at the boys hand and winced. "You got him good, didn't ya?"

Mandy giggled from her spot next to her brother. "He hit the floor and wiggled around for a minute before getting back up."

Liam couldn't help it, the giggle was contagious. He laughed with the two of them.

"Did you two even eat yet?" he asked, glancing at the dashboard clock.

They both shook their heads no. "Well c'mon then. Let's get y'all some lunch."

Slowing down against traffic, he signaled and pulled into Donna's Country Store. The three of them walked into the building together and went up to the counter, checking out what was in the hot case. "Looks like we got pizza rolls, slices, and maybe some chicken wings," Liam mumbled. "What do you want?" he asked, looking at Drew.

"A couple pizza rolls."

He motioned to the cashier behind the counter to grab those for Drew. "And what do you want, darlin'?"

She wrinkled her nose at the pizza. "Can I get a sub?" she asked, eyeing the menu board of sub sandwiches.

"Yeah, whatever you want."

The kids' eyes widened. Those words hadn't been spoken to them in a very long time. It dawned on Liam that Denise probably hadn't been able to do this for them, and they were unsure what they were allowed to get. Perhaps they didn't feel comfortable asking him for something. Tapping the counter, he went down the aisle and grabbed two bottles of soft drinks and a large bag of chips. He added onto that a couple of chocolate bars, because he figured everyone liked chocolate bars. Once back to the counter, he ordered a sub for himself for good measure. When the total came to over $20 he saw their mouths drop open.

"It's okay," he assured them, pulling his wallet out of his pants. He laid a couple of bills on the counter and waited for his change. "Drew, why don't you go clean up a little bit in the bathroom," he motioned to the men's restroom.

With Drew gone, he and Mandy stood holding their purchases in silence. He had absolutely no idea what to do with a girl, and the silence was awkward.

"Can you make sure Drew doesn't get in trouble?" she asked him out of the blue.

"What do you mean? He's already in trouble at school."

"With Momma. She's gonna beat his butt. I just don't think it's fair. He was protecting me, and if he gets in trouble, then I should too."

They reminded him so much of him and Roni that he had to smile. "I'll take care of it. I promise."

"You keep your promises don't you?"

She looked at him so shrewdly, he blushed. He didn't want to lie to her, ever. "I try to," he answered honestly.

Reaching over, she hugged him around the waist. It took him by surprise, but he hugged her back the best he could with the bags in his hands.

Drew came out of the bathroom looking much better, and they all went and got in the truck. As they drove back to the shop a song came on the radio, and Drew turned it up, he and Mandy singing along. Unable to help himself, Liam sang along too. Never before had he wanted to accept someone else's kids as his own. But these two were special, and he would never forget this being the first day he'd ever thought of himself as a father.

Chapter Fourteen

"**D**enise is back."

Liam didn't want to admit that those words made him happy. He'd been worried about her. It wasn't a dangerous mission they'd sent her on. It should have been an easy in and out, but that didn't change his feelings where she was concerned. He didn't like using outsiders to do jobs that members of the club should do. Though he knew that since he'd claimed her in front of the club they would expect her to work for them – it still didn't sit well with him.

On top of all of that, he now had to explain that her son was suspended from school. A doctor that did favors for the club examined Drew once they got back to the clubhouse, and now the twins were playing out back with the other kids. The boy had been quiet for the most part since they left the school, and it had worried Liam. The doctor assured him that everything was fine.

All talk stopped as Denise strutted through the front door of the clubhouse. The only time any of them had ever really seen her was when she was dressed as a frumpy mom of two teenagers. This woman that walked through the door was a damn siren.

"I see that," he mumbled as he gave her a slow, leisurely once over.

Her hair had been cut and it looked highlighted. The clothes she had on hugged her body. Who knew she had curves and legs that went on for days? The skirt she wore showed those legs and hugged her ass in the most amazing way. Makeup made her eyes look huge. This woman was living in his home?

"Hey," she greeted him softly, looking uncomfortable as she noticed all eyes on her. Her voice was a little deeper than normal, her accent just a little thicker. She sounded like a porn star talking to him about everyday life. "I got what you need."

He cleared his throat. He was sure what she said and what he heard had two totally different meanings. "I'm sure you do."

Brows furrowed, she gave him a look that said blatantly she hadn't meant what he had heard. "What? I got the property records."

Pissed at all the attention she was getting and the feelings he was having, he stood up and put his arm around her waist. "Why don't we go talk about this in the office?"

"I'm fine out here," she argued.

"No, trust me, we need to go to the office," he instructed. As they walked away, he threw a glare at all the brothers still watching the two of them.

When he finally steered her in the right direction, he shoved her into the office and slammed the door on the laughs that followed them.

"What was that all about?" she asked, folding her arms over her chest.

The motion caused the shirt she wore to tighten and showed the cups of her bra through the thin material. He had to shake his head when he realized that piece of fabric was the only thing between his eyes and her naked body. "You have no idea do you?"

"I'm so lost, Liam." The tone of her voice told him just how much. "Didn't I do what you wanted me to?"

"You look hot!" he blurted out, causing heat to gather on her cheeks.

"Oh," she mumbled, pressing her hands against her skirt. Men didn't say things like that to her, and it immediately gave her sweaty palms. "You can thank Sparkles for that."

"Shut the fuck up. What were you doin' with Sparkles?" he asked, laughing loudly.

She bristled. "I couldn't figure out what to wear. I called your sister, she called Sparkles."

"Don't go gettin' all uptight on me, baby. You look great. I'll have to let Sparkles know how much I appreciate it."

"You do that. Do you want to see what I found or not?" she asked as she had a seat and crossed her legs.

He groaned. She wore nude hose with the fuck me heels she also sported. This was a turn of events he had not expected. Not from the person who only acted like a mother. He wondered if she slept in the nude. Shit, he was going to hell – quickly.

"Liam?"

"Yes, what did you find out?" he barked, much harsher than he meant to.

Her eyes were clear as she looked at him. They didn't show fear, but they did show concern. "Are you in a bad mood?"

"More like hornier than a motherfucker," he mumbled.

"What did you say?"

He had a seat in the chair behind the desk, spreading his legs to give his ever expanding dick a little bit more breathing room. "Nothing, I'm fine. But before we talk about what you found out, we gotta talk about Drew."

"What about Drew? I had a message from school earlier, but I didn't have a chance to call them back."

"Drew got into a fight today."

Her face reddened with anger, and her eyes widened. "He did *what?*"

"Now, don't get mad. Just hear me out."

"Hear you out? Why did they even call you?" she asked, fuming.

"Because *you* put me down as an emergency contact."

She realized that he was right. "I'm sorry, I'm not thinking clearly. My son was in a fight? Is he hurt? Was the other boy hurt? What were they fighting over?"

"This is where I need you to hear me out, Denise."

Taking a few deep breaths, she tried to slow the pounding of her heart when the instinct was to run to her child and make sure he was okay.

Liam could see her looking out the window to the office, obviously trying to get a look at Drew. She was such a better mother than the one he'd had. Clearing his throat to stop his show of emotion, he soldiered on.

"Drew and another boy got into a fight over some pretty graphic and lewd comments made to Mandy."

"Oh my God, are you serious? She's thirteen years old," she gasped.

"I know. And Drew did what any brother would do for his sister, he stood up for her. The other boy was suspended for six days, Drew for three. I don't think he should be punished. He's such a serious kid as it is."

He worried that he was overstepping a boundary here. He was essentially giving her advice on how to raise her children. Something she'd done on her own their entire lives. Her reaction to this would tell him just how ready she was for a relationship. Which, in turn, brought about the question he had to ask himself. Was he really ready for this? With her it wouldn't be fuck and run. It would be waiting on the front porch with a gun when boys came to the house to pick up Mandy for a date. It would mean giving Drew the birds and bees talk – taking him to his first strip club when he turned eighteen. Instead of feeling panicked, he was completely calm. That, more than anything else, told him that he was ready for this.

"I know," she worried her lip between her teeth. "He is serious, and I'm thankful that he stood up for Mandy. I'm worried about him, but I'm not mad now that I know why he was fighting. I think you're right."

"Mandy will be happy to hear that," he grinned at her.

"Why's that?"

"She told me that if Drew got in trouble then she should too because he was standing up for her."

Denise laughed. "Those two have always stuck together – since they were little babies. I think this is an exception we can make. This one time. I do want him to know that I won't tolerate fighting."

"I think that's fair," Liam agreed.

An awkward silence enveloped them. They had just spoken like parents of two children or maybe a married couple. It was a little disconcerting.

"Anyway, back to the information you got for me."

She leaned over, grabbing the USB out of her purse. As she bent, the neckline of her shirt fell down, exposing breasts that were cupped by silk. His earlier thoughts wondering about what her naked skin looked like were gone now, replaced with wondering if her nipples were sensitive or not.

"Damn," he breathed.

"Did you say something?" she questioned as she straightened back up and reached over to hand it to him.

He cleared his throat and let his eyes caught the lacy edge of the bra she wore beneath her shirt. "What? No, let me see what you got."

He told himself to get his head in the game and pay attention to what she was talking about. Taking the USB from her, he let his fingers brush against hers. It sent a flash of awareness through his body, no other woman had ever affected him like this. With a sigh, he put the USB into his laptop and pulled up the file.

"I noticed that the deed was quit claimed about three months ago."

"What does that mean?" he asked, loving the sound of her voice. It showed in her inflection that she took an interest in what she had done.

"It means they didn't go through a bank. The terms of the sale were agreed upon by both parties and done by a lawyer for a small fee. That means it doesn't have to be approved by a bank, and there doesn't have to be any financing. When I pulled up the LLC's name, it showed me they have ten more properties in the Barren County area. All of them were quit claimed three months ago by the same person."

"Who was it?"

She went behind the desk and reached over his shoulder. He didn't move when her chest came into contact with his body as she leaned over and grabbed the mouse. Liam watched as she clicked a few buttons to sort the document and then chose a search option. "Umm, looks like a Richard Joyce owned all of them before the quit claims."

"Son of a bitch," he cursed slowly. That cooled his desire off like no amount of cold water could. The club had a history with this man.

"You know him?" she asked.

He laughed harshly. "You could say that. Dick, as we like to call him, is a former member of the club and dad's ex best friend. He's not even supposed to be around this area."

"So it's bad he owned these buildings?"

"It's bad that he's got his grimy paws on whatever the shit this is. Thanks for the information. I gotta talk to William about this."

Gone was the carefree guy who been openly flirting with her a few minutes before. Here now was a man who looked like he could commit cold-blooded murder. The quick change of mood was the one thing that scared her most and made her question the decisions she had made.

Chapter Fifteen

enise squirmed, uncomfortable. She had made dinner only to have her children decide they wanted to eat with new friends. After their day at school, she figured they deserved a little bit of time with people who wouldn't judge. This meant that she and Liam were left alone in his house. Because she'd already cooked, he'd decided to eat with her. It had been a quiet affair so far.

"Have I done somethin' to piss you off?" he asked, taking a bite of his baked potato.

She looked up sharply. "No, why?"

"Since I talked to you earlier, you seem like you're either pissed off or scared of me." He shrugged, rattling his ice in his glass before taking a drink. He watched her closely. It was obvious she wanted to say something, but she held back. "You can say whatever you want to me, I won't be mad."

"Are you sure?" she asked, playing with the food on her plate. "Because earlier, you went from a happy-go-lucky guy to looking like you could murder someone with the flip of a switch. It scares me. I have children in this home with you."

Silence settled over the two of them, so obviously at different points in their lives. Liam thought over how he should answer her. He debated over whether he should tell her the truth or tell her what she wanted to hear. It hurt him to know that she worried about her kids with him. Had he not proven he respected not only her but the kids? Hadn't he proven that just today?

"Don't lie to me, please," she whispered.

"That's just me."

That didn't make her feel better at all. "What do you mean that's just you?"

"I *am* that guy. I go from 0-60 in two seconds. I can be your best friend or your worst enemy. That's who I am." His stomach dropped as he saw the look on her face. For some reason he wanted to impress this woman, and apparently his answers weren't cutting it. Never before had it mattered to him what a woman thought of what he did. Now, nothing else mattered but what this woman thought.

"Oh."

Panic welled up in his stomach. In all his life, he'd never scared a woman, and he was confused as to how he had scared Denise. "Don't do this, don't be scared of me."

She got up from the table and walked to the screened-in porch. Hugging her arms around her waist, she looked out into the black of night. Lightening streaked in the distance, and light rain hit the tin roof that covered the porch. The storm building in the atmosphere matched the storm building inside her.

Was she doing the right thing? Should she stay in this situation with this man? Was she too far in to get out? The big question….did she want to leave? For some reason she felt safe in this environment. Much safer than she had felt when she was on her own with her children. It was all so confusing. Denise felt him enter the small area but refused to turn around and face him.

"You're not used to me and I know that, but you're going to have to get used to me. I've claimed you. If you leave me, which I can tell you're thinking about doing, you'd have a bull's-eye on your back. I know you don't want that for your children." He felt like a bastard for even saying those words.

She finally turned to face him. "It may sound weird to you, but I feel safe here. In the few days I've been here I've felt more at home than I did when I was in my own home. Maybe it's because I don't have much to worry about here. The only thing that worries me about you, Liam, is the fact that I don't know how far you would go for your club."

"What do you mean by that?" he asked, having a seat on the outdoor chaise.

Denise didn't want to ask this question because she didn't want to know the answer, but she felt as if it was imperative that she know. "I mean, have you ever killed anybody?"

He swallowed hard. Telling her the truth would mean letting her in on club business, but lying to this woman would break his heart. Liam sighed. Lies were a part of his everyday life, but he didn't want to lie to her. He wanted whatever relationship they had to be built on trust.

"I could lie to you and tell you I haven't, but I want you to trust me. I do what I have to do to keep my brothers safe, to protect my club. That has at times meant we've had to put someone down. More than once it's been either them or me. I don't like telling you this because I know it scares you about me, but I'm not a violent man by nature."

"I don't like violent men," she whispered, gazing at her hands in her lap.

She looked so lost that he wanted to reach out to her. However, he wasn't sure whether she would welcome it or not. He'd know this woman for mere days, but it felt like forever. They seemed to be cut from the same cloth, yet he knew that she would never be able to kill someone unless they threatened her children. How could he come to her as he was? With blood on his hands?

Gently he questioned, "Did something happen to you?" Suddenly it dawned on him. "Does this have to do with the twins' dad?"

A hollow laugh echoed from her throat. In the distance, thunder rumbled and lightening flashed across the sky. "You could say that."

"It's only fair that you be honest with me, just like I've been honest with you."

Taking a deep breath, she realized he was right. "Their father was a very violent man."

"Trust me enough to tell me, Denise. We're never going to get anywhere if you don't. I'm not letting you go back home, so you may as well just be honest with me. I can't let you – it could be dangerous."

She liked this about him, the fact that he was so tenacious. That he didn't take no for an answer. It tested every instinct she had honed over the last few years. Tears came to her eyes, and she cleared her throat loudly, gathering the strength to begin.

"I met him in high school, senior year to be exact. He was the captain of the football team. I had always been a nerd. More interested in what book was coming out that month than anything else. Books were the most important part of my life at that time. I was painfully shy, and my home life left a lot to be desired. My dad stayed drunk most of the time, and all my mom wanted to do was stay out of his way. He was violent when he drank, and if I had my nose buried in a book, I could stay under the radar when he went off the handle." She had zoned out as she talked, it was obvious she had transported back to that time. The rain sounded against the house, just like it had that night. Only it wasn't hitting the tin roof of a trailer, she was now in a home that was well-built and cozy.

"So when the captain of the football team started showing you attention, you were flattered?" Liam supplied for her.

She nodded, tears silently streamed down her face. "But you have to understand how horrible it was at my house."

The breath she took was heavy and fragile all at the same time, almost like it would break her in half. A loud clap of thunder rattled the house on its foundation. "I walked on egg shells all the time, trying to do what both my mom and dad wanted me to. Matt, the kids' father, was the answer to my prayers at first. He took me out on dates, took me out to dinner, brought me flowers, and told me he loved me. He invited me to prom, and I finally told my parents we were dating. Miracle of all miracles, my parents told me to go. My dad liked the fact that he was captain of the football team. It was something for him to brag about at the bar when he got wasted. We had been dating for a few months by the time prom rolled around, and I thought that night was going to be incredible." She stopped, took another shuddering breath, and composed herself.

"Let me guess, prom night wasn't all that you'd hoped it would be?"

A sad smile spread across her face. "Let me finish. After we spent an amazing night dancing with friends, he told me that he had a surprise for us. He took me to a hotel room. I lost my virginity in the most amazing setting. He was so gentle. It was everything I had always dreamed of. The next day everything changed."

"How so?" Liam wasn't sure he wanted to hear this, but knew he had to.

"He became possessive. If I wasn't home when he expected me to be there, he was pissed. He would scream and yell at me to the point that he and my father came to blows one night. It was the first and only time my dad ever stuck up for me. If I had a male friend, Matt would try to intimidate them. I started withdrawing into myself again, and two months later I found out I was pregnant."

Liam could guess how it had gone when she'd shared that news with the daddy-to-be. "Matt wasn't excited was he?"

A hollow laugh came from deep within her. "That's the understatement of my life. I was tainted goods, and Matt didn't want the responsibility he was now going to have. Ole Daddy wasn't too happy either. The night I told Matt, he beat the absolute shit out of me. Of course I had to tell my dad what happened. Instead of being understanding, he kicked me out."

He grasped her hand, running his hand along her wrist. "It hurts when a parent isn't understanding, I know."

She nodded, sobbing as the rain came down in sheets outside. It had been on a night like this that she had walked miles, trying to get someone to help her. "I mean, here I was an eighteen year old kid who just found out she's going to have a child and who just had the shit beat out of her. I went home expecting my parents to be pissed but hoping that they would welcome me with open arms and tell me that everything would be okay. Instead, my dad packed a bag for me. Me and my broken ribs were thrown out into the mother of all thunderstorms. Kind of like the one tonight."

"How did you survive?"

"How does anyone survive? They just do."

He had tears in his own eyes as she recounted her story. Denise Cunningham was the strongest person he had ever met in his life. "You had no help. That's what's surprising to me. You had twins with no help." The people who should have cared, they didn't even give a damn.

"I relied on public assistance for a couple of years. Then I got the job at the factory. That was the most money I had ever seen in my life, and we were able to live very comfortably up until the economy took a nosedive. I was proud of how far I had come, but the downturn caused me to question everything. I had worked so hard to provide for my family, and then we had nothing to show for it besides a stack of bills and a mortgage I couldn't pay."

"You should still be proud of how far you've come and what you've done. Everyone has hard times; it's how we deal with those hard times that define us."

In that moment, she wanted badly to kiss him. To show him physically how much those words meant to her, but it had been so long since she had kissed a man. She was nervous that she didn't remember how to do it.

He made up her mind for her when he gently brought his hand up to cup the back of her neck. His fingers lightly massaged the muscles there before he pressed lightly and leaned towards her, bringing them closer. Their lips met in a light touch. He was patient as he coaxed her lips open before slipping his tongue inside her mouth.

She moaned, placing her arms around his neck, pulling him close. Her tongue stroked his tentatively, as she contemplated what to do with her hands. She had wanted for so long to run her fingers through his hair. Throwing caution to the wind, she let her fingers tangle in his long locks, using it to pull him tighter against her lips. It was as silky and smooth as she had imagined it would be, sliding against her fingers as she fought to hold him tighter.

Moments later they separated, both breathing heavily. He kept his hands at her neck while she continued to twirl the strands of his hair around her fingers, a shy smile breaking over her face.

"That was nice," she sighed, running her tongue over her wet lips.

A thought occurred to him, causing him to smile widely. Crow's feet broke at the side of his eyes, evidence of the hours he spent on his bike squinting in the wind and sun. "Is that the first kiss you've had in all these years?"

Suddenly shy, she buried her head in his neck. "I was raising children," she defended, her protest muffled.

He laughed. "Well Denise Cunningham, I think it's about time we get you back to the land of the living."

Chapter Sixteen

"You'll need to wear this," Liam instructed, handing Denise a helmet.

This was the first time the two of them had ridden his bike for pleasure, and she was a bit nervous. She put the helmet over her head and made sure to strap it at her chin. The night before, when he'd told her it was time for her to join the land of the living, she hadn't thought he meant so soon.

"This is going to be much different than last time, huh?" he joked.

"No, I loved those bullets flying past my head," she deadpanned.

He got on and motioned for her to slide on behind him. When she did, he grabbed her thighs and pulled her so that every inch of their bodies touched.

"When you ride bitch, we touch."

The tone of his voice sent chill bumps up her spine, and she gladly scooted up so that she could wrap her arms around his waist. She made sure to snake her arms under his cut, as close as she could get. The feelings of a new relationship made her want to be as close to him as she could. As they rode she held on tightly, leaning this way and that with his body. They came to a stop too soon. Excitement shot through her as he brought his gloved hand up to rest on hers. It was fleeting, but it was one of those small touches she'd never had before. This whole situation made her feel like a teenager dating someone for the first time. It was new, exciting, and she loved it.

"*This* is what you meant by getting me back into the land of the living?"

Liam laughed as he swung his leg over the back of his bike and helped her off. "I'm gonna assume you've never been to a strip club before. So yeah, this is the land of the living."

Her eyes were wide as she gazed upon the building in front of them. *Wet Wanda's*, the neon flashing sign proclaimed. It was an old building, built in the sixties or seventies vein, and looked like it was built with rock. It was so old the rock looked gray. An hourly motel sat adjacent to it.

"I'm not so sure about this," she mumbled as she grabbed his hand and followed closely behind.

The bouncer at the door knew him, and Liam lifted his chin in acknowledgement, grasping the bouncer's hand and shaking it. She barely listened to the words they exchanged, but she was curious when the bouncer waved them in, not even asking for a cover charge.

They entered the belly of the beast, and she couldn't help but glance around. It was dark in the main part of the building, but she could see that it was very clean. A large stage dominated the room which separated into individual stages amongst the floor with booths around them. Scantily clad women raced back and forth between tables hauling food and drinks. Among the people she could see some of the members of Heaven Hill. She wondered just how often Liam and the guys frequented this establishment.

"You alright?" he asked her.

She nodded as he led them to a booth further back in the room. From there they had a good look at the main stage. In front of them, the table blocked most everyone from looking at them. The vinyl of the leather was clean and comfortable. It was obvious that it was well used, but it was in good condition. Sinking deeply into the booth, she snuggled up close to him. His arm went around her shoulders as he got comfortable. Spreading his knees, he braced his feet on the floor, giving the impression that he was just a man there with his woman.

"I'm okay, this is just different," she explained, trying to avoid looking at some of the more provocatively dressed women.

A woman walked up to their booth, this one a little bit more covered up than the rest. "How you doin' Liam?" she asked, giving him a polite smile.

"Not too bad, Bianca. Can I get a beer? Whatever you've got on tap."

"And you honey?" she glanced expectantly at Denise.

That caught her off guard, she wasn't a big drinker, and she had no idea what 'tap' meant. "Sure, same here," she blurted out.

Liam laughed. "You're not a drinker are you?"

Her face flamed in embarrassment. "I haven't really had time to do that."

His hand stroked her shoulder, causing goose bumps to break out on the skin exposed there. "Do you like Sprite?"

"Yeah."

Bianca could see where he was going with this. "Do you like Strawberries?" she asked, her eyes twinkling at the exchange between these two.

"They're my favorite," Denise admitted, wondering if she'd get herself some strawberries out of this.

"I'll hook you up with something a lot better than a damn beer. I'll be right back, y'all."

Once she was gone, they sat in silence. Liam took in what was going on in the club, and Denise wasn't sure of how she should act now.

"You come here often?" she blurted.

"In my youth, yeah. Now we work protection for the club. Someone is here every night. We make sure the ladies get out of here safe, and if there's any problem in here, we take care of it. Most of the women working here are trying to make better lives for themselves. Bianca, our waitress, is in college. She's damn smart."

Before she could say anything, the woman they were talking about came back with their drinks. She sat a drink down in front of Denise. "Try that and tell me what you think."

It was clear, with strawberries in the bottom. It looked carbonated, but she wasn't sure what this was. Looking at the two of them, she took a sip from the small straw that sat in the drink. It had a bit of a bite, but it went down smooth. "That's good. What is it?"

"Strawberry flavored Vodka and Sprite. Be sure and let those strawberries sit in the bottom and then eat 'em, but watch it. They'll be completely full of alcohol."

Bianca left them to go to another table, and Denise went back to sipping on the drink.

Liam took a drink himself and removed his arm from around her shoulder. "You're gonna have a good time tonight," he predicted.

The smooth burn of the drink kept going down her throat and her tongue opened up, telling him things that she hadn't told anyone else ever. She told him about how lonely she'd felt being the single mother of twins. Bianca kept bringing the drinks. Denise was on number three when she shocked the hell out of him.

"Oh, and have I ever told you how sexy you are? You have this dark, dangerous look about you and the tattoos going up and down that one arm," she leaned forward so that her lips met his ear. "They get me hot."

"Holy shit woman, you've got to stop drinking now." He immediately realized how much the alcohol was affecting her. It was nice, but he didn't want her this way.

He motioned Bianca over. "Hey, get her some water, coffee, something else besides alcohol." His teeth were clenched, and Bianca laughed, knowing exactly what was going on.

Underneath the booth, her hand rested on his thigh and then curiously went further up, grabbing his package with a firm grip.

"Whoa, whoa, whoa," he breathed loudly through his nose. "Don't start something you won't finish here. With you, I'm a hair trigger," he warned.

For the first time, his guard was completely down with her. She gazed into his eyes, seeing the honesty there. He was trying so hard to be a gentleman, to show her that he was different than the only other man she had ever been with. Pulling her hand back, she let it rest on his thigh again.

"Is that okay?"

"You can do that."

Bianca came back, putting a mug of coffee in front of her, along with some milk, cream, and sugar. Her mouth opened to say something, but it was drowned out by the screams of the crowd that had gathered as the lights went down.

"What's going on? Am I going to see a woman strip?" Denise asked, doctoring her coffee cup.

Liam smirked. "You seem like you might like that, which surprises me, but no. Not tonight. Jagger's performing."

Jagger Stone was a Prospect in the club. She'd seen him a few times. They'd said 'hi' and 'bye' when they had passed at the club.

"Performing?"

He nodded. "He sings, plays guitar, and writes songs. He's damn good."

Bianca had stood still at their table, watching as Jagger took the stage and had a seat.

"She always watches, but she never admits she has a thing for him," Liam pointed at Bianca. "They haven't ever even exchanged 'hellos', that girl is so shy."

Denise could relate. Now that the alcohol was wearing off, she was embarrassed by the way she had acted.

An hour and a half later, Jagger wrapped up his set and threw a guitar pick out in the audience. She had to giggle as two women fought over it. With startling clarity, she realized that many women had given Liam the eye as they walked past him. If she wanted to live this life, she was going to have to learn to take what she wanted. If she didn't, there would be someone there to scoop this man up if she let him go.

"Let's go, it's gettin' late," Liam said low in her ear.

They got up and left the club, walking into the warm, muggy night. Once at his bike, he handed her the helmet she had worn on the way over. Before putting it on, she leaned into his body, wrapping her arms around his waist.

"Thanks for this. You're right, I've never done anything like this before, and I had a great time."

He brought his hand up to her cheek and brushed her hair out of her face. "You're welcome. Next time, we'll go a little bit lighter on the booze huh?"

She giggled, still feeling a little loopy from it. She blamed that for what she did next. Standing on tiptoe, she crushed her lips to his, sweeping her tongue against the opening of his mouth. When his hands tucked into her hair, she pulled away and got on the back of his bike.

Getting on the front, he felt her arms wrap around his waist, and he took a moment to put his hands on her thighs and squeeze. It was a comforting gesture and she loved it. Turning his head over his shoulder, he kissed her once more before starting the bike and heading off into the night.

Chapter Seventeen

Two days later, Liam sat at the clubhouse while the group tried to figure out what exactly Richard Joyce had to do with their rival's business. They had brainstormed since Denise had provided them with the intel. Deciding to take a few days to do some reconnaissance, they were now back to speculating about Joyce's involvement.

"What the fuck does he even do now?" Tyler asked, cracking his knuckles and frowning as he thought about the man that had once been their brother.

"Good question,' Liam praised him. "Steele, work your magic."

The group sat back for a few minutes, allowing the computer expert to do what he did best. If there was anything in the world that could be found out about another person, Travis Steele would find it.

"Huh, what the fuck do you know?"

"Do share with the rest of the class," William said as he walked into the clubhouse and had a seat next to his son. He had been scarce since the evening he spent with Lauren, knowing that Liam would be uneasy about it.

"He's in the banking industry."

"What the fuck, someone gave him access to money?" William laughed. "He had a gambling problem when he was a member. Wonder how he passed that background check?"

"This is even more interesting. He's got calls placed to someone we all have in common. Meredith Rager."

The group groaned. "I am so sick of her," Liam complained, running a hand through his hair. "If I never hear that name again it will be way too fucking soon. Speaking of which, Tyler don't forget, we got to go sign off on that class so that we don't have to go to court on those bullshit charges."

"I'll go do it tomorrow. So what's the connection?" Tyler asked, trying to take the heat off of Meredith. For some reason he liked the nosey reporter, but he didn't need to tell everyone his feelings.

Travis raised an eyebrow. "It's also the same bank that Denise uses. I'm beginning to think he's watching deposits and alerting the reporter as to who we may have working for us. Didn't you say that reporter paid Denise a visit after we gave her the money for helping us out?"

"But what would that do for him?" Liam asked. "Let's talk this out. What's he doing this for? What's his motivation?"

"Trying to play both sides of the coin? He's involved with us since he's watching deposits at Denise's bank and presumably feeding Meredith info. He's involved with the Vojnik because he purchased land for them, then quit claimed the properties to them." Tyler tried working it out.

"Good question, maybe Ms. Rager knows," William interjected.

"Let me go talk to her," Tyler said, looking at the group as a whole.

Everyone looked at him uncomfortably. Tyler was a force to be reckoned with and one of the most physically dominating members of the club. No one wanted to cross him or piss him of. Liam could see the looks on the faces of the other members.

"Why don't you and I take a walk Ty?"

Tyler nodded, and the two of them got up, walking outside for some privacy.

"I don't want to hear whatever shit you're gonna spew at me," Tyler threatened.

"I am your vice president. You will speak to me with respect or so help me God, Blackfoot, I'll knock your motherfuckin' teeth out. Best friend or not. You be careful with this woman. I know you've got some sort of misguided hard-on for her, and I'm not sure why. You make her understand that working against us will cause her nothing but trouble. Do you understand?"

The Native American ground his teeth together. He hated being reprimanded, especially by his best friend. "I got it."

"Make her understand, because neither you nor I can protect her if she goes down. You know that as well as I do. If she's fucking around with us, she's fucking around with them. I think we're the least of her worries, but at the same time, I don't want her blood on our hands."

Tyler nodded and headed for his bike. He knew what his VP said was true, not only speaking as the VP but as his friend. He just wasn't sure he could make her understand. She was hungry for the attention and recognition that exposing the two clubs would bring her, and that was dangerous.

Meredith sat in front of her laptop, pencil in her mouth as she wrote her script for that night's newscast. This one was pivotal. She would be exposing secrets of the two clubs, and this was sure not only to put her on the map but to put a bounty on her head. She thought she was ready for whatever it brought her – even if it meant the end of her friendship with Denise or a bullet to the head. A knock on her door sounded, and she cursed loudly, locking the laptop before getting up and answering it.

"What the hell do you want?" she asked Tyler as he pushed his way inside.

"This is the last time I'm gonna be able to warn you, and you better take it fuckin' seriously. Whatever you have on us and the Vojnik, you forget. You are going to get yourself on the bad side of a lot of people. I'm telling you now, you are going to get hurt."

Her heart pounded in her throat, but she couldn't let him see her sweat. "Why are you warning me?"

His dark eyes flashed as his mouth sat in a grim line. It was obvious even to her that he had feelings for her, she just wasn't sure what they were. "For some reason, I feel responsible for you. I feel like maybe I shouldn't have used the information you gave us. I think you're a beautiful woman who has a head for what you love to do, but you're walking a dangerous line, Meredith. Some of these men are cold-blooded killers, and they will snap you in half if you so much as look at them wrong. You have no idea who you're messing with here."

She appreciated his warning and she even appreciated him looking out for her, but she had to do this. It was not only her job, it was her pride in that job being done well.

"It's my job to report the truth."

"Who told you it's the truth? How do you know? Tell me what information you have, and I'll tell you if it's the truth." He was very close to begging, something he never did.

"You'd like that, wouldn't you? You'd like me to tell you everything I know so that you can use it to your advantage. I'm not whoring myself out for your club, Tyler Blackfoot. You want to know exactly what I have? Watch the 6 o'clock news. I'll be reporting it then."

He closed his eyes and fisted his hands. He wanted to shake her and scream at her to think. These were men who had served hard time. They wouldn't think twice about hurting or killing a woman. Throwing his hands up in the air, he turned around because he couldn't bear to face her anymore.

"I can't protect you once this news hits, I'm warning you of that right now. I have to do what my club tells me to."

She wanted so badly to tell him the secrets she knew. He really was a good guy, and in another life they may have dated. He, with his larger than life personality and movie star good looks. They appealed to her, and if she wasn't who she was and he wasn't who he was, they really may have made a go of it.

"I'm not asking you to protect me, but I appreciate the sentiment."

"Then so be it. I've done everything I can think of to warn you off of this. I've done my duty. When you get scared, don't call me and sure as hell don't ask for my help."

Those words made her want to cry. He really was writing her off. He was giving up on her. "I won't."

The two of them gazed at each other for long moments before he grabbed her hand, bringing the back of it up to his lips for a soft kiss.

"Be careful," he warned.

"You too."

She stood at the door, watching him leave. It felt final, and that scared her. Had she just made the biggest mistake of her life? Shaking her head, she went back to her story. It no longer held the promise of her fame. It now seemed like it would be the gunshot that would take her to her grave.

Chapter Eighteen

"**B**reaking news tonight at 6. Investigative reporter Meredith Rager exposes outlaw biker gangs in and around South Central Kentucky."

Denise felt sick to her stomach as she sat with the group of bikers, and probably over half the town, ready to tune in for what was promising to be a big announcement. Tyler had let her know that he'd gone earlier to warn Meredith, to let the woman know that whatever she *thought* she knew was probably not the truth. Denise's heart sank when he told her that Meredith had blown him off. They hadn't been great friends, but Meredith had been a neighbor, and she genuinely liked the younger woman. This had *bad* written all over it.

"Doesn't seem like you did your job too well, brother," William reprimanded as he glared at Tyler.

"That woman is a bulldog. I did what I could. She's bound and determined to have her body sliced apart and stuffed in different dumpsters around the county. Who are we to stop her?"

Liam knew by looking at his friend that not being able to talk her out of this had upset him. It had cut deeper than the big man let on. Tyler kept his feelings very close and hardly ever let anyone in. As well as they knew each other, there were still some times that Liam didn't really have a good bead on him.

"You know where this is headed."

The woman's face they were talking about appeared on the television screen. Tyler could tell she was nervous. It was evident as he looked in her eyes. She bit her bottom lip as she waited for the cue that would let her know it was her turn to begin speaking. He could see the fear in her eyes, the uneasy way they darted back and forth between the teleprompters.

"Thanks, Brent," she smiled shakily at the co-anchor for the night. "A year-long investigation into local outlaw motorcycle gangs - the Vojnik and the Heaven Hill MC - has revealed many shocking secrets."

Collectively, the group watching the newscast leaned forward, almost as if they could hurry her along. They were just as eager as the general public to learn the info she had.

"Many will remember the body of a man that was found by a natural gas crew laying new pipeline earlier this year. News Center can exclusively reveal that man's name and who is taking credit for the murder."

On screen, Meredith stalled and took a deep breath. This had all seemed so easy when she was researching and writing it. Now, she felt as if her heart was about to beat out of her chest, and she had a bull's-eye painted in the middle of her forehead. Her hands shook as she shuffled her paperwork, and it was on the tip of her tongue to lie about the information she had sitting in front of her. No one would really know, she argued with herself. But it was her job to be truthful and to report the news.

"The body was that of prominent Bowling Green businessman and city councilman Jeffrey Norris who went missing fifteen years ago amidst reports he was taking bribes from the Heaven Hill MC."

As those words left her mouth, there was a loud explosion, and the screen went black.

Silence reigned over the group for a full minute as they processed what they had seen before they all jumped up and began talking at once. Over the excited chatter, William's authorative voice rose.

"Turn that goddamn police scanner on."

Fumbling to do as he said, Steele turned it up so that they could all hear.

"Dispatch to all essential personnel, there has been an explosion at News Center studios. I repeat, an explosion at News Center studios. Injuries are unknown, fatalities are unknown, damage is unknown. Everyone must report. Local hospital is on alert!"

The enormity of what had just happened sank into the group and Liam looked at Denise. "We have club business to discuss, you gotta go."

Tears clogged her throat. This was scary business, and she had no idea what was going on. She wasn't sure who she was more worried for, Meredith or Liam. "Do I go home or wait for you outside?" she asked, her speech thick with fear.

"You can go wait for me at home. Call Roni and get her to come keep you company. I'll walk you out," he said softly, trying to soften this turn of events.

He wanted to punch someone, he was so pissed. She had just told him that she felt safe, and they had just had a good night out. And now this shit? He prayed this wasn't a deal breaker for her.

"I'll be right back," he told the club as he took her hand and walked them out to where his truck sat.

She cursed herself because she still relished the feel of his hand on the small of her back. In reality, she knew she should be scared to death. These men had just been revealed to her as killers. It was weird, she still felt safe in this setting. She wasn't sure if that would ever change.

"This wasn't us," he whispered softly as he turned her around to face him. She leaned against the driver's side door of his truck and crossed her arms over her chest.

"Really? Because right now, it seems like it is." Her eyes searched his blue ones, hoping to find the man she knew, not the one who needed to go deal with a bombing. She knew he was in there, and she wanted him to take her into his arms and assure her that everything would be okay.

"I can't explain this to you right now, but I will when I get home. I promise you that." He was making promises and almost begging – this woman had him by the balls.

Denise kicked herself mentally because she knew she sounded like a petulant housewife. "And when will that be?"

A heart stopping grin plastered itself on his face. "Do you realize just how much you sound like an old lady right now?"

That pissed her off. Was he inside her head now? "The hell I am."

"The hell you aren't. Get used to it."

A million horses couldn't stop the smile that spread across his face as he put her in the truck after kissing her on the forehead. Tapping the hood, he sent her on her way before going back inside to deal with the shit storm that had just landed at their feet.

Minutes later, Denise pulled up to the house. For the first time, she felt fear. They had left a light on, and she glanced up the porch through the front door to make sure it was still shining brightly. Noting that it was, she breathed a sigh of relief.

Jogging up the stairs, she checked in on the kids who were both asleep in their beds. That was a huge weight off her shoulders, to know that they were safe.

On her way home, she'd placed a call to Roni, and the other woman was coming over. It was late, but she knew with all the excitement of the day there was no way she'd be able to sleep. Grabbing a book she had been reading, she took herself to the screened-in porch and had a seat. All she had to do now was wait.

A lit cigarette in his mouth, Liam made his way back to the clubhouse, sighing as he realized they faced a complete fuck fest.

"So who fed her the bad info?" he asked as he took his VP spot at the table.

"My money points to ol' Dicky boy. He must have a back end deal with the Vojnik. He's trying to get us out of the way."

It was well known between both clubs that none of them had killed Jeffrey Norris. His wife had caught him with his pants down one time too many. She had come home early from a vacation with their children, and she'd caught him banging his new secretary. A woman scorned, she'd had enough, and after the mistress had left she'd shot him in cold blood. For a hefty fee, Heaven Hill had helped her dispose of the body, but they sure as hell hadn't killed him.

"I say we go down to the station and see what's going on. With it exploding right as she revealed our 'huge secret', heat is gonna be on us," William groaned. "Which is exactly what we fucking do not need, but exactly what they want."

Chaos reigned around her as Meredith fought to climb out of the black hole she'd fallen into. Her head hurt, and her tongue felt heavy. In the distance she could hear police sirens and people screaming. It took a great deal of strength, but she fought to yell at them, to let them know she was there and that she was okay. In the end the climb was too hard, too long, and she just gave up. Tyler had warned her this would be the end of her, and maybe he had been right.

Chapter Nineteen

"So, how's it going with my brother?"

Denise's head snapped up from where she lay lounging on the screened-in porch with Roni. Since Denise had already been out there, that's where they had decided to stay.

"Good," she answered a little too quickly, her voice a little too high pitched.

Like a hound dog on the scent of a kill, Roni sat up straighter, grinning wildly. "He's gotten to you, hasn't he?"

She did not under any circumstances want to talk about this. Telling him that she hadn't had sex in thirteen years was embarrassing enough, but to tell his sister...she wasn't really down for all of that.

"Gotten to me?" she played dumb.

"Whatever. My brother is a good lookin' guy. I know that. The two of you in this house every night, I'm sure you've gotten...close."

"First of all, we aren't in this house every night. I think we may have spent two nights in this house together, that's it. Second of all, I'm a mother. I take care of my children most of the time. There is absolutely nothing sexy about that. In no way has he 'gotten to me'."

"You doth protest too much."

Roni knew that Denise was worried. She'd heard it in her voice when Denise had called to ask her to come over. What better way to distract her than to talk about sex?

Never having what one would call a gossipy girlfriend before, Denise was out of her element. Was it okay to talk to other women about this stuff?

"So we had a 'moment', but it was *not* sex. Trust me." Her face burned a bright red, giving her completely away.

"Oh do tell." Roni clapped her hands together, excited for her brother and her friend.

"It was just a couple of kisses."

"*Just* a couple of kisses? The way you're blushing, that must have been some kiss."

She cleared her throat and took a deep breath. "To be honest, even though I am a mother I don't have a lot of experience. He just makes me nervous. I mean I'm sure he has women all over the place."

"I could lie and tell you that my brother is a saint, but he's not. Just give him time, he'll bring you over to the dark side," she giggled, eyebrows raised.

Denise wasn't sure exactly where the dark side was, but it went without saying that she wanted to experience it.

"Post club members at every exit of this hospital, nobody gets in or leaves that we don't know about," Liam instructed as the MC went about damage control.

One of the policemen on their payroll had already conceded the police presence that was supposed to be posted outside of Meredith's door. Tyler now stood there, daring anyone who walked by to say a word to him. The nurses openly flirted, the doctors just put their heads down and continued on about their business. It was very evident that he would be okaying anyone who went through that door.

"Liam, I need to have a word with you."

He groaned. He knew that voice and he didn't want to have to deal with this right now. "What Rooster?"

"Where were you and your club tonight?" he asked, casually resting his hand on his gun belt, and looking the other man in the eyes.

Liam hated when he rested his hand on his gun belt. It straight up pissed him off. "Not that I have to tell you. If you really had something, you'd be arresting me so fast my head would spin, but I'll do you a favor since we go so far back. We were at the clubhouse, watching the news like everyone else in this town."

"And you know nothing about the explosion that did heavy damage to the news station?"

Liam grinned sarcastically. "You've known me for years. Have I ever been a goddamn explosives expert? Has anybody in my club ever been?"

"Cut the bullshit, this is serious. I'm asking you a serious question. This is huge. The FBI has been called in on it. You and I both know that you don't want the FBI or ATF sniffing around. And Layne's ex Special Forces. Be honest with me, for once in your life."

That pissed Liam off. "You know what Rooster? I've always been honest. I've always been me. You're the liar wearing a goddamn badge. You wanna ask me anymore questions, you contact my attorney. Oh and by the way,

Layne's a Prospect. If we did this our names would be all over it, motherfucker."

Office Hancock glared at his one-time friend. "You stay available."

Glaring right back, Liam got his word in. "You stay the fuck outta my way."

Muffled voices sounded like they were miles away. This was the third or fourth time Meredith had heard them. Each time, she tried with super human strength to acknowledge them. Each time, she failed. This time though, her resolve strong, she fought against the pain she felt. It was as if she was coming up for air to keep from drowning. As she broke the surface she gasped, sitting straight up.

"Calm down," hands pushed her shoulders, pinning her against the bed. Those same voices took on soothing tones as they began speaking to her.

"Meredith, you've been in an accident. Can you remember anything?"

She shook her head as she opened her eyes. The light was bright and a group of people stood above her. Recognizing doctors and nurses, she began shaking. *What the hell happened to me?*

"You're going into shock Meredith, keep looking at me," one of the doctors said, keeping eye contact with her, trying to soothe her.

"What kind of accident?" she managed to stutter out, her body shaking so much her teeth chattered.

"There was an explosion at the news station. Do you remember anything?"

Just like that, she was out again.

It had been a long night. Liam yawned as he stood with a group of members that were manning one entrance. They had seen neither hide nor hair of any Vojnik members, which just reinforced the feeling that Heaven Hill had been set up.

"VP, why don't you head home?"

Liam glanced up at his dad. He looked just as tired as Liam felt, but he knew the old man was waiting for something, anything to happen. He expected Richard Joyce to show up, and he would be there when he did.

"If you're not goin' home Dad, I'm not goin' home."

Placing an arm around his son, William brought him close. "It's an order, go home. You're dead on your feet, and you need to check on things there. If that ass has targeted the reporter, he may have targeted the other women as well. I mean let's think about how Denise came onto our radar."

Liam had to admit the old man had a point. It could have been coincidence, but it also could have been orchestrated by the former member. He knew without a doubt that Denise wasn't involved, but knew it wasn't out of the realm of possibility that she be a pawn in whatever sick game he appeared to be playing.

"I'll have my pre-pay on. Call me if you need me."

The sun was beginning to rise on the horizon as he pulled into the driveway of his home. Even summer mornings were a little chilly as the morning dew gathered on the surface of the earth. He felt raw; Richard Joyce had been an important member of the club. His brother, just like the rest of them. Liam worried now about Denise and her children. If Meredith had been set up so badly, what could Joyce do to children if he got it in his mind to do so?

. His thoughts were dark and heavy as he parked his bike and made his way into the house. It was quiet at this time of morning, eerily quiet for him now. It was funny how quickly he'd become accustomed to having two teenage children living there. If he was being honest, it hadn't been a home until he had people to share it with.

Walking up the stairs, he checked on both kids before walking to his bedroom. He rolled his shoulders. They were tight with the tension and stress the night before had placed on him. It hurt him that women had been targeted in an all-out war against his club. Against him. It pissed him off, and when he got ahold of Richard Joyce he would kill him with his bare hands.

Moments later he was in the shower, letting the scalding hot water wash away his anger, his disappointment. He felt like all of this had been laid at his feet, and it was expected that he would scoop it up and put it on his shoulders. Liam knew that he could take it, but first he had to come to grips with it. First he had to admit he'd brought this to his own front door.

"How could one of my own brothers have been this bad?" he whispered, pushing his hair back from his face.

This was his responsibility as VP, and he knew it. Therefore, he would take care of it. It would take him to a place he didn't relish going. A place he didn't want to go to with Denise living in this house with him. This though was for his club, and he couldn't back down. Hell, he wouldn't back down. Richard Joyce had fucked with the wrong man, the wrong club.

Getting out of the shower, he dried off, securing a towel around his waist. Exhaustion washed over him, and he looked forward to the bed that was awaiting him. Running a hand over his cheek, he contemplated shaving, but the bed sounded much better.

Walking out of the bathroom, he scrubbed his head vigorously with another towel. When he decided it was as dry as it would get without a hairdryer, he dropped the towel into his hamper and turned towards the bed. What he saw stopped him dead in his tracks.

"What are you doing?" he asked, his voice complete gravel with lack of sleep.

She stood in the middle of the room, a short t-shirt barely covering her panties. Her hair lay haphazard against her shoulders, and she had the lazy look of sleep in her eyes. Running her tongue along her bottom lip, she smiled softly at him.

"I talked to your sister tonight. I'm ready to take a walk on the dark side."

Chapter Twenty

Struck stupid seldom happened to Liam Walker, but it sure as fuck happened when those words left her mouth.

"The dark side, huh?" he grinned slowly, the words flowing out like smooth bourbon.

Her stomach fluttered as she looked into his blue eyes. They were warm with affection and something dangerous as he looked her body up and down. She realized that she stood there for him like porno flick brought to life.

"The dark side," she confirmed. "Although my dark side and your dark side might be two different things," she giggled softly.

She watched, her eyes wide, as he grabbed her hand. Pulling her up alongside his body, he turned to face her.

Reminiscent of their first kiss, his big hands framed her face and held her in place as his mouth bent down towards hers. When their lips touched, she brought her hands up to grip his biceps, hanging on for dear life. He invaded her personal space, crowding her against him as his mouth ate at hers. Arousal bloomed in her stomach, stronger than she'd ever felt before. Unclasping her hands from his biceps, she ran them down his pecs and the muscles of his abdomen. Encountering the towel, she stopped.

"It's your decision," he whispered as he pulled his mouth away from hers. Her lips were swollen and wet, evidence of just how badly he wanted her.

Excitement ran high on her cheeks, and she knew without a doubt that she didn't want to stop. She wanted something for herself for once in her life. Denise wanted to be a woman again. Not just a mother, but something beyond that. Biting her lip, she moved her fingers to the tucked end of the towel and pulled. Unabashedly, she watched as it sank to the ground. Heat rose on her cheeks as she saw the evidence of his eagerness.

"Don't get shy on me now," he pleaded, bringing her flush with his body. He knew he couldn't give her time to think about what she was doing. If he did, it might be over before it began.

Running his hands down her neck and around to her back, he let them trail down to her ass and cup it as he picked her up. She squealed slightly as he lifted her. "Put your legs around my waist," he instructed gruffly.

This was new for her. As a teenager, sex had always been in the backseat of a car or hurried when they got a few minutes alone. She'd never been picked up before, and it was exciting. Threading her fingers through his hair, she used it to keep her balance, pulling slightly.

"You like pullin' my hair baby?" he asked, his voice dark and sinful.

"I like your hair. Period." She admitted.

He brought her higher up onto his body. She watched with appreciation when his biceps bulged. Her interest captured by the movement of his muscles, she didn't see him tilt his head down. When his mouth came into contact with her t-shirt covered nipple, she gasped. The cloth of the cotton made it feel forbidden and muted the feeling just enough to excite her. It made the touch feel almost nonexistent but put her on edge because it made her want more.

"More," she begged.

With gentle lips he rolled the nipple before clasping his teeth around the hardened flesh. She rewarded him with a sharp intake of breath, and he moaned at her response. The soft moans coming from her mouth drove him crazy. Tightening her fingers in his hair, she pulled his head closer and then buried her face against the side of his neck. His fingers tightened responsively on her ass as he felt her tongue along the tendons of his neck. As she nipped his throat and earlobe, he staggered slightly. Grinning to herself, she swiped her tongue along his ear, gripping the hoop earring he wore there with her teeth and tugging slightly.

"Damn," he swore darkly. "I'm ready to throw you down on this bed and fuck you raw, but you deserve so much better than that."

Her breathing more ragged by the minute, she shook her head, shutting her eyes tightly against the sensations he evoked in her body. "No, that's what I want," she panted. "It's been thirteen years, Liam. Thirteen long, lonely years," she pouted, her hand sneaking down behind her to grasp his erection.

He threw his head back at the sensation. Her soft hand was small and held him tightly. When she rubbed her thumb across the tip, she gathered a drop of the wetness there and spread it down the length of his hardness. "I don't wanna hurt you," he ground out, teeth clenched.

"Just do something," she pleaded.

She had him to the point of violence, and he knew he had to get rid of some of it before he rutted on her like a bitch in heat. He made sure her legs were locked around his waist and then let go of her before bringing his hands up to the top of her t-shirt. Fusing their mouths together again, he ripped the collar and tore it right down the middle of her body before doing the same with the panties she had somehow managed to keep on. He had lost control, he knew it and was beyond the point that he could regain it.

Tossing her on the bed, he took a minute to take her in. He knew that how she looked at this moment would always be imprinted in his brain. The way her hair lay haphazardly around her body, the sweet way her legs splayed open for him, the hardened tips of her nipples, pink with the irritation from his teeth. This was an image he never wanted to forget.

"Wait," she stopped him as he grasped her hips and brought the center of her body closer. "I'm not on birth control."

Liam couldn't believe he hadn't even questioned that. "Shit, sorry," he apologized. "I'm usually much smoother than this, but you are one fucking hot piece of ass," he complimented. She gave him a beautiful smile as he reached over to the bedside table and grabbed a condom.

Within moments, he was suited up and ready to go. She watched as indecision suddenly flashed in his eyes.

"It's gonna hurt regardless of how wet I am for you, Liam. It's been thirteen years, but could you please just put an end to my drought?"

He threw his head back and laughed. That was what he'd needed, something to break the seriousness of the moment. It was all too serious, all too life changing, and he knew it. Carefully, he took himself in hand and rubbed the head of his hardness over the nub of her clit, gathering the moisture that lay there. He prayed it would make it better for her.

"Ready, baby?" he asked as he perched himself at her entrance.

She nodded bravely, letting him know that this was so much more than sex. He could see it in her eyes. There lay a trust he hadn't seen before.

Crying out as he pushed in, she bit her bottom lip, tears coming to her eyes. "Just breathe," he instructed as he leaned more heavily on her, grasping her hands in his. Carefully, he retreated and then pushed back in as he let his tongue caress her nipple again.

He could feel her relaxation as he gradually moved back and forth. When she wrapped her legs fully around his body and dug her heels into his ass, he knew that she was okay. Throwing caution to the wind, he rocked into her body, picking up speed when she gripped his hands harder.

"Oh my God," she panted. It had never felt like this before. She'd never had this feeling of flying, this ache that felt so good.

"C'mon baby," he encouraged, pulling his lips away from her nipple. Bringing his finger up to her mouth, he instructed. "Lick it."

Her tongue wrapped around it, just as he'd asked. She wasn't sure what he was going to do, but she watched with wide eyes as he brought that finger down to where they were joined and she felt him begin to strum her clit. The moan she let loose was music to his ears, and the tightening of her body told him that she was about to let go.

"Don't you want to feel it? It's been so long," he coaxed her through.

The orgasm hit her body like a semi. Realizing she was going to wake up the kids if he didn't quiet her down, he put his hand over her mouth as she rode it out.

"Son of a bitch," he gasped when her teeth bit into his hand. She was the hottest thing he'd ever seen.

Crushing her body to his, he thrust once, twice, three times before burying his head in the crook of her neck and moaning his release.

Both lay panting, a maelstrom of emotions swirling, when his pre-pay rang on the bedside table. He cursed, not wanting this to end, especially so soon. He knew though, he had a job to do.

Chapter Twenty-One

"I gotta get this," Liam apologized. He hated that the club was interrupting this moment, but this was his life. Her life now, if she would have it. It was a wakeup call that she would have to face sooner rather than later.

She understood, so she nodded, but damn did she resent that phone. Rolling over, she pulled the covers tightly around her body and listened. He hung up and turned so that he spooned her from behind, nuzzling his lips in the crook of her neck.

"We gotta go," his voice was still deep and slow with the relaxation of their previous activities.

"We?" she asked, closing her eyes. Denise wanted to soak up whatever time she had to enjoy this. It had been so long since she allowed herself to enjoy the closeness of another human being, and she didn't want it to end.

"Meredith is awake and she's not being very forthcoming with the information that we need. Dad seems to think that you may be able to talk to her."

Allowing herself a moment, she snuggled up to him, shivering as his hand gripped her hip and flipped her over. She ran her hands over his chest when he leaned over her, capturing her body with his. Their lips were inches apart, and she wanted to beg him to kiss her again, to let her feel the slow sweep of his lips, slide of his tongue.

"I don't know why he thinks she may talk to me. The last time we said words to each other, she warned me away from y'all."

He grinned before kissing her softly on the lips. "Well, I see the two of you seem to take advice right about the same way. I'm glad you ignored hers."

"Me too," she agreed, even though it was soft and he almost couldn't hear her. She still wasn't exactly sure just what she had gotten herself into.

When they arrived at the hospital, Denise gawked at the number of bikes parked outside. Liam had told her the whole club was on the lookout, but she hadn't thought he truly meant *everyone*. This group even looked like it included other clubs since she observed colors and patches that weren't familiar to her.

"These aren't all Heaven Hill members are they?"

He shook his head, grabbing her hand as they made their way up to the entrance. "Not all, no. There's about three clubs here that are friendly with us. We don't have enough members to make this large of a showing."

Feeling shy because his club witnessed them walking up together, Denise fell in step behind him, waiting for the ground to eat her up. Her face heated because she was sure everyone could tell just by looking at her what they had been doing.

He refused to let go of her hand, causing her to turn her palm so that she could keep up with him. Approaching the group, Liam called out to his dad.

"Anybody showed up?"

The older man took a drag off the cigarette in his mouth, shaking his head before blowing out a steady stream of smoke. "Nothin'. I figured somebody would at least do a drive by, you know, to see what's going on. If they have, we haven't seen them. Tyler's kept everybody but doctors and nurses out of the reporter's room too, so she should be up for a visitor," he threw a pointed look at Denise.

"I'll do what I can," she promised, tightening her grip on Liam's larger hand that held hers. William scared her – he was so different from his son - she did not want to be on the business end of his fist again.

Liam saw the uncertainty in her eyes as she gazed at his dad. He understood, because sometimes he was just as scared as she appeared to be. Liam pulled her body even with his and put his arm around her neck, tugging her securely to him. "Dad, she's not a miracle worker. Back off."

"We don't need a miracle worker here, we just need to know what the hell's goin' on."

"And we'll figure that out, just give us some room to work," Liam brushed past his old man and dragged her along with him.

"I don't want to get hit by him again," she whispered as they made their way down the hall.

He growled, looking back to where William still stood outside the main door to the hospital. "He ain't touchin' you again. It'll be alright. You get us what info you can, and we'll work from there."

They had arrived at Meredith's door, and Tyler stepped aside to let her enter. Searching for strength reserves she didn't know she had, she took a deep breath and walked inside.

Denise had never been in many hospital rooms. The only time she'd ever had an overnight stay was when the twins were born. It looked much different than she remembered. Meredith lay in a bed that looked five sizes too big for her. There was dark bruising on her face and her wrist was wrapped in an ace bandage.

"Are you okay?"

Turning her head to face her visitor, Meredith ran her tongue along dry, cracked, lips. "Yeah, I guess so."

This was not going to be easy. Apparently the reporter didn't like to admit when she'd fucked up.

"Who did this?" Denise tried again.

"Would you believe me if I told you I don't know? I have a contact at the bank, but I don't know his name. In fact, I'm only assuming it's a man. He covers up his voice. He's the one who got me an in with the Vojnik. I might as well have written my own death warrant tonight."

She winced as she situated herself higher in the bed. While she hadn't' been hurt too badly, soreness marked almost every inch of her body.

"Why didn't you listen to Tyler? He tried to tell you not to do this."

Anger flashed in Meredith's eyes. "Why didn't you listen to me? Besides, how do I know *he* didn't do this?"

"C'mon, we were all at the clubhouse watching the news when you started talking and the explosion happened. If he was going to do this, why would he warn you? I think we both know that he has more than a passing interest in you. Don't be stupid, he's standing outside that door, not allowing anyone in just to keep you safe."

"Why isn't Tyler letting people in? Why is it so hard to believe that he did this? He did warn me, but what if the warning wasn't that? What if it was a threat?" Meredith wrapped her arms around her waist. "I don't know *who* to trust at this point."

Denise couldn't argue with her logic but knew for a fact that the bombing was not Heaven Hill's doing. "I hope you know what you're doing, Meredith. You're a good journalist, and a decent person, but messing with the stuff you are is going to get you hurt worse?"

Trying very hard to keep her composure, Meredith spat back. "Is that a threat?"

"No. Anyone with half a brain can see where this is going. Is being famous and having that ten o'clock job every night worth all of this?" She gestured to the hospital room and bed with her hands. "You have some person feeding you information about *outlaw biker gangs*. There's a reason they're outlaws. They don't play fair. You're a pawn, and they're using you to the best of their ability. Do you want to die?" Denise pleaded with her. Surely she was smarter than this.

"No," she whispered. "But now I don't know how to get out," she admitted. "I know so many things, and I don't know if any of it's the truth. I know that this was a play on

Heaven Hill now, but I didn't before. It had to be to set them up for something they haven't done, and I don't know who did it. I have too many informants, too many contacts."

"Do you need protection?" Denise asked, feeling weird about asking, but she felt like it was her place to assume, her place as an affiliate with the club to offer.

Meredith thought about the big man who stood guard at her door since she'd been brought in. She wanted him and only him to protect her, but with him came the rest of them. Now wasn't the time to show anyone just how scared she was.

"No," she whispered, tears brimming in her eyes.

"I'm going to tell them what you've told me. It's some guy at a bank."

"I know."

Denise wanted to shake her. It was obvious Meredith wanted help, but she'd be damned if she asked for it. "Do you have anything else you can give me, Meredith? These guys will protect you if you give them a reason to."

Sighing deeply, she reached her hand out. "My purse is over there under the chair. One of the EMT's brought it to me."

Denise handed it to her and waited, impatiently rocking back on her heels. She wanted this over as quickly as possible.

She pulled out a manila envelope, somehow salvaged from the explosion. "This is the information my contacts gave me. I don't want it anymore. I can't stop what I've already started, but maybe I can keep it from getting worse."

Denise walked out, envelope in hand. "She gave me what info she has. I'm not sure what's useful to you, but maybe we can start trying to figure out who's setting the club up and why."

Liam kissed her forehead. "Thanks for getting this for us, I know it's not easy to do this kind of stuff. We really appreciate it. I appreciate it more than I can tell you." At his hip, his pre-pay buzzed, he flipped it open and read the text he had just received. Cursing loudly, he ran his hands through his hair. "We need to figure this out now."

"What's wrong?" Tyler asked, concern etched on his face.

"They just picked up dad. Steele says they're takin' him to county lock-up. I'm heading to the clubhouse. You stay here and watch over Meredith. Denise you come with me. Whoever has decided to make us an enemy doesn't know what match they just lit."

"Be careful," Tyler called out.

If there was one thing Liam Walker didn't stand for, it was someone shitting on his club. Now that they'd picked up the president, Liam looked ready to kill.

Chapter Twenty-Two

"Rooster, you got nothin' on me," William appealed to the young man he'd known since birth. "What you have is a bunch of circumstantial bullshit."

"Pretty good bullshit though, even you gotta admit that. We have Tyler Blackfoot at Meredith's house hours before the newscast. What she said implicated your club in the death of a prominent citizen."

Grinning, William interrupted, "We are Harley enthusiasts."

"You wanna talk about some bullshit? That's the biggest load I've heard in a while. You're fingerprints are all over this, William."

"Then show me. Where are they? What can you pin on me? Because if you can't, then cut my ass loose."

Rooster got up from his chair and walked over to the door. "You know what? I think we might have some more questions for you. I can legally hold you for twenty-four hours, and I think that's what I'm going to do. Maybe I can even dig up an old warrant."

"Fuck you, Rooster."

"My name is Officer Hancock, don't forget it."

William smirked. "Don't forget who you're talkin' to."

"I could say the same to you, old man."

When the door closed, William slammed his head on the table. This was turning into one hell of a clusterfuck.

"They should be setting bail or releasing him within the next few hours. Until that happens, there's really nothing we can do."

Liam sighed as he got off the phone with Lee, the club's attorney. It sucked having your hands tied. He'd called Roni and let her know that their dad had been picked up. Now he sat at the clubhouse trying to make sense out of just what in the hell was going on.

"So, Lee says it's gonna be a few more hours on the old man. Let's try and see if we can make heads or tails out of the information Denise got from Meredith."

"I think we can safely assume that the man feeding her this load of shit is Richard. The question is, why? What's in it for him?" Steele asked, taking a drag off his cigarette. "I hate to say this, but you know who could probably tell us?"

Liam didn't want to hear this. "Aww fuck you, not right now. I can't deal with her right now."

"I think it's time we call your mom."

Lauren Walker was and always had been a sore spot for Liam. The betrayal and hurt of her leaving was a wound that still festered in his chest every time he allowed himself to think about it.

"If we call Lauren, it's gonna be my sister talking to her. You know I can't stand her."

He knew that Roni was outside with Denise watching the kids. Before he asked her to do this, he had to get his emotions under control. Every time his mom was mentioned, he felt like a little kid again. He'd watched her leave that day, and he'd screamed through the door begging her to come back. Not once had she turned around and looked at him. With a sigh, he lit a cigarette and made his way over to where the two women sat.

"I need a favor," he directed to Roni as he had a seat in between the two of them.

"You always need something. Why should this be any different? What do you want?"

"I need you to call Lauren."

"Are you ever going to call her 'Mom' again?" Roni asked. This was a point of contention between the two of them. She had somewhat forgiven their mother, he wasn't sure he ever would.

"Look, don't give me any shit," he snarled. "I don't like asking you to do this, but you and I both know I can't talk to her."

"Can't or won't?" she challenged.

Denise looked between the brother and sister, wondering just what had gone on with his mother that caused him so much pain. Behind the harsh words, she could see the eyes of a little boy. She'd seen those eyes on her own son when he spoke of the father he'd never met.

"What do you want me to ask her?" Roni asked, giving in like she always did.

"Thank you. We need to know what exactly Richard had to do with Jeffrey's death. Obviously he knows something, but I want to know *how* he knows. This was supposedly kept strictly among club officers, and he never was one. Dad had a gag order in place on that shit. Do we have a leak here? Is it a bigger problem than what we think?"

"I'll call her and let you know what she says. Why don't you go home and try to get some sleep. By the time we put all of this together, Dad will be out – hopefully. Denise why don't you go with him? I'll get the kids to help me clean up the clubhouse. Ya know, keep them outta your hair for a while."

Liam couldn't help the shit eating grin that broke across his face. Reaching down, he grabbed Denise's hand and pulled her up beside him "Let's go."

Hours later, they lay in what had become her favorite place at Liam's house, the screened-in porch. A blanket covered them as they lounged just enjoying the quiet and each other's company. She could hear his deep, even breathing which told her that he slept soundly. It was the first time she'd seen him sleep since she'd moved in. It seemed like he was always on the go, always doing something for the club.

When she wondered what he liked to do for fun, what his favorite foods were, and what he normally wore to bed at night, she realized just how little they knew about one another. It made her want to know everything about him. He sighed deeply, snuggling her up in his arms.

"Hey," she greeted, smiling softly. "Did you sleep good?"

It surprised him, but he had. "Yeah, I did. I guess I needed it." Stretching, he leaned forward, kissing her lightly. "Has my pre-pay rang?"

"I didn't hear it, but I fell asleep for a little while myself."

He reached over the side of the chaise, where he had thrown his jeans and pulled the cell out of the pocket. "Shit," he breathed when he saw three missed calls and a voice mail.

"Everything okay?"

Putting the cell to his ear, he help up a finger and pressed the buttons to listen to the voicemail. After a few moments he put the phone back in his pocket and leaned back against the bed.

"Dad's out of jail, and Roni's interrogating Lauren as we speak. She's taken the kids over there, hoping to soften the old witch up, then she's taking them for the night. Darlin', looks like we have a night to ourselves. What should we do?"

Lying back down, she bit her bottom lip between her teeth. She knew what she wanted to do but wasn't sure if he would go for it. Inspired, she sat up, pulling the blanket tighter around her body. "I have an idea."

"I'm all ears, I need a relaxing night."

"One of the many things I've had to put off because of my kids has been dating. I haven't been on a date in years. Do you think we could have one?" she asked, biting her nail nervously.

"Will you dress up for me and do your hair and makeup and all that shit? Ya know, look like you did the other day when you did that job for us?"

He seemed so excited, she couldn't help but laugh. "Sure."

"Then I'm giving you an hour. You better be down here ready to go. You want a date, baby, you got yourself a date."

Gifting him with a gorgeous smile, she got up, holding the cover around her and leaving him in the nude. As she stepped over and around his body, his hand smacked her ass and she shrieked playfully.

"Is that a preview?"

Eyes darkening, he chuckled. As she ran up the stairs, he called after her. "It can be."

Chapter Twenty-Three

The smell of hairspray caused Denise to cough as she finished her hair. She was trying desperately to make it look how the hairstylist had made it look. Taking her hands to it, she artfully mussed it, smiling at the end result. She had never been good at hair or cosmetics, but tonight she wanted to be. Unlike most nights, she had also taken great care with her makeup, hoping that Liam took notice.

Walking over to the bed, she glanced at the outfit she'd laid out for herself. Sparkles had convinced her she was wearing clothes two sizes too big, and she had to admit Sparkles had been right. Smoothing her hands down the shirt she wore, she blew out a nervous breath.

"What the hell, Denise. You only live once right?" she whispered to herself. This was the time to make the changes she had wanted to make for years. Liam was giving her that option, and she knew that she'd be crazy not to take this opportunity and run with it.

Liam sat on the couch in his living room, twiddling his thumbs. He didn't think he had ever been so keyed up in his life. Excited didn't even begin to describe his feelings at this moment. He felt special. This wasn't some woman who was a friend of the club, she wasn't a hanger-on just looking for a good time. A quick fuck in his dorm room so that she could go back and tell all the other women how big his dick was. This woman was actually upstairs trying to look cute for him. In all his years, he'd never had what one would consider a girlfriend, much less an old lady. He'd just had a couple women here and there in his life who had warmed his bed, and that was never for long. He always got out before it got too serious, before they started demanding his time and requesting words he didn't want to say. This was just as new for him as it was for her.

When he heard the click of heels against the hardwood of the stairs, he glanced up. A low whistle sounded from his lips as he got a good look at her. She blushed, smiling softly as she descended.

"Look at you," he admired appreciatively, the low rasp of his voice showing just how much he liked what she wore and the care she'd taken with her appearance.

Turning in a circle, she spread her arms out so that he could get a decent look at her. It was unusual, to feel on display like she was. She watched as his eyes roamed her body, from the top of her hair to the stiletto boots that encased her feet.

"You, Denise Cunningham, are lookin' like sex on a silver platter right now. Believe that."

It was true, his eyes had almost popped out of his head when he first caught sight of her. A pink tank top hugged her curves while a pair of boot cut jeans showed off toned legs. She wasn't what one would call tall, but the jeans and shoes made it look like her legs went on forever. It was amazing how confident she'd become in the days they'd known each other. He was watching her blossom, and he loved it. In the back of his mind, he wondered if he was hindering her as much as helping her. Once she got in too deep with the club, there would be no getting out. Shaking those thoughts from his mind, he smiled at her.

"Thanks, I do feel kinda good about myself in this," she admitted, walking over to where she had laid out a black leather jacket.

She put it on and looked at him for approval. "Do I pass biker bitch inspection?"

The grin on her face showed that she was teasing. He liked this playful side of her. When they'd first met, he wouldn't have known she had such a sense of humor or such a bangin' body. Both were *very* pleasant surprises.

"You pass *old lady* inspection," he clarified.

"What does that mean?"

He forgot that she wasn't familiar with biker lingo. She hadn't been born into the culture, and many things were still foreign to her. At that moment, he realized just how much he *wanted* her to be a part of this culture.

"It means kind of like a wife without the ring. I can get you a 'property of' patch, which means you're my property and no one messes with you without facing my wrath."

"Can I think about that?" She wasn't really sure what all this entailed, even though he'd just explained it to her. She would need to speak to Roni about what he had just proposed.

"Of course," he answered, even though it hurt his pride to know that she couldn't make a snap decision like that. "You ready to go?"

Excitement danced in her eyes and bounced off her body in waves. "Yes. Where are you taking me?"

Her excitement fueled his. He'd never felt this way about taking a woman out before. "Out to dinner, then we're taking a nighttime ride. It's beautiful to ride at night.

"Awesome, I can't wait."

An hour later, they arrived at a local steakhouse and were seated. She couldn't help but notice that people watched Liam as they walked by. There seemed to be many different schools of thought about this man that had come to mean so much to her. Some looked at him with thinly veiled fear, some looked at him with a glaring respect, and the women looked at him with undisguised lust. Her mind raced. She wasn't sure if it was because of him personally or because of the club and outlaw life he represented. Either way, it made her uncomfortable to see other women look at him that way. Scooting closer to where he sat, she made sure their legs touched and that everyone could see it.

"Would you like to sit on my lap and feed me?" he joked as she slid over one more time. Accommodating her, he moved his arm up on the booth and put it around her neck, pulling her closer to him.

Denise had the decency to blush. "These women looking at you just pisses me off."

A deep chuckle sounded in his throat. That was great to hear. "You got nothin' to worry about," he reassured her.

The two of them had put in their order and now sat talking softly over their drinks, a bottle of beer for him, a margarita for her. Out of the blue, she blurted, "What's your favorite color?"

"I'd have to say whatever color your underwear is," he flirted, taking a pull off his beer.

She preened prettily, huffing at the same time. "I'm serious here. We know nothing about each other, but we're living together and you've asked me to be your old lady. Do you not see anything wrong with this?"

His large hand enclosed hers, and he brought it up to his lips before turning it over and placing a soft kiss on the pulse point at her wrist. "I know all I need to know. You love your kids, you're loyal and honest. You know that I love my family, my club, and I'll always protect you. What else do you need?"

"It's not conventional," she argued.

"If you haven't noticed this about me yet baby, I'm not conventional. If I have a feelin' in my gut, I'm goin' with it," he quirked an eyebrow at her. "And to be honest, you aren't really conventional either. Don't let society's rules about what's conventional make you uncomfortable with what we do."

"Is that how you do everything in life?" she asked.

"For the most part. I'll admit to you that it sometimes bites me in the ass, but when it works out it's usually the best time of my life."

Denise yearned to be like him, to just let things fall as they may, but she had her kids to think about. "I'm a mom," she explained.

"I realize that, honey. And I promise you this, no matter what happens between us your children will always be taken care of. Just let this happen. We may be together forever."

"And we may not."

He brought his hand up to her cheek. "And we may. What's life without risks?"

"Comfortable."

"Tell me," he begged, leaning his head into her neck, nipping her ear. "Do you want comfortable? Or do you want this out-of-control feeling we get whenever we touch each other?" he breathed, causing goose bumps to pop on her arms.

"The out-of-control feeling," she whispered, relenting to the feelings he evoked within her.

It was hard on her though, leaving everything up to chance. A part of her conscious argued that her carefully laid plans had backfired on her before. Why not do what she wanted to for once in her life?

"Do you wanna take the long way home?" he asked after dinner. They sat on his bike, waiting for her to fasten her helmet.

"Yes," she agreed. Anything to allow her to keep her arms around him and hold on tight. Riding the bike with him had become her favorite pastime and one she didn't want to give it up anytime soon.

He cranked the bike and revved it, causing her to dig her nails into his cut before they took off onto Scottsville Road. He eased into a lane of traffic that would take him onto the interstate and allow him to hit the back roads that would take him all the way to his house.

As they stopped at a light, he leaned into her. Reaching his hands up, he caressed hers where they rested on his flat stomach. He snuck a kiss through her open-face helmet, groaning when her hands moved down further to the apex of his thighs.

"Not here baby, it's hell ridin' with a hard on."

She threw her head back and laughed. It felt good to be free with him. To do everything that she'd always thought about doing but had never been sure she would ever get to do.

The light changed, and they raced off into the night.

Chapter Twenty-Four

"So I talked to Mom last night. To see what she had to say about Richard."

Liam groaned. He really didn't want to talk about club business, especially not after the amazing night he'd had with his lady. However, he knew this was important. There had to be a reason that Richard was looking into framing the club, and he needed to know why.

"Do tell."

"According to her, there was a power struggle at one point between him and Dad. During that power struggle, Mom says that she and Richard got close. What she meant by that, I don't know. She wouldn't go any deeper into it than that. She did tell me that Richard wanted to break off into his own charter, and Dad wouldn't approve it. They had a protection run for Jeffrey Norris. Apparently he was skimming off the top of the books for the city and buying black market electronics. He would in turn sell them on the street for a straight profit. That money then came back into the drug trade. Mom thinks that Jeffrey and Richard had a back-end deal with said drug trade. Jeffrey supplied the money, Richard supplied the drugs. When I asked Mom what she thought about why he wanted to pin this on us right now, she thought it might have something to do with bonds on a life insurance policy."

She stopped, letting this all sink in. It was obvious that Liam was having a hard time processing.

"A life insurance policy? This is an awful lot of bullshit to hand out to a lot of people for a motherfucking insurance policy." He couldn't believe it was as simple as that.

"With Jeffrey's body never found, they couldn't have him declared dead. He's been a missing person. Since Richard's been buying up all this property and buildings, she figured his cash reserves are being depleted, especially since he's not earning with the club anymore. Apparently, Richard is the beneficiary on one of Jeffrey's policies because of their back-end deal. Mom thinks, too, that at one time they may have been trying to go legit together – that's neither here nor there. His name is on a life insurance policy, she knows that for sure. If he can get the money and hurt the club at the same time – why not? There's also all that land the club owns out on Highway 185. You know people have been trying to get it for years, they think it'll make a great housing community. If the club gets taken down, then he could have a legal right to it. He was here when the club started. I'm sure his name is on the deed to most of that land. Mom offered to check on it for us, since she works at the courthouse."

The information took a while to sink in, and when it did Liam cursed. "So this isn't some spur of the moment bad decision on his part. He's thought this through."

"Exactly. We need to be on our toes."

"What about the reporter? Where does she fit in all of this?"

Roni shrugged. "Collateral damage? I think she was just a pawn, and she's talked to a few too many people. I'm a little scared for her. My thought on it is he used her to figure out who we were using, to gain himself an ally. When that didn't work, he just started playing with her. Now he's fed her bad information, and he knows for sure she's shared it. In his eyes she's a narc."

"We can't worry about her. She's made her bed, she'll have to lie in it," Liam dismissed Meredith's role in this.

"You wanna tell your bff that? Tyler is so far into that girl I don't think he knows where she ends and he begins. We have to warn her. She really could be in trouble and being cute is not going to get her out of it. These people could *really* hurt her."

"Fuck," he hissed. "I'll call him and let him know. Tell him to give her a heads up. I have a feeling that 'special report' was nothing but a set up on their part."

"I hate to say this, but you may wanna warn Denise too. Just because *we* don't hurt woman doesn't mean they don't."

He groaned. "We just had a motherfucking conversation about keeping her safe. This would have to happen now."

"Maybe we should do a lockdown for a few days. Until you can find Richard and find out exactly what he's doing. I mean, he's gonna be sticking close by. As soon as that report comes back and gets filed, he's going to petition the court. You can bet your ass on that."

She had a point. It appeared Richard wouldn't stop until he got what he wanted, and that meant money and blood on his hands. "I'll talk to the old man."

Meredith was beginning to feel uneasy. Her body was still sore from what it had gone through in the explosion, and now her contact from the Vojnik was running late. He was never late. This wasn't exactly the best part of town to be in, and nerves were starting to make her stomach queasy. Pulling the jacket she wore tighter around her body, she paced by the river that flowed through the outskirts of the city. She stood under a bridge that most teenagers used for prom pictures, but she didn't feel any of that lighthearted carefreeness at this time. At night this turned into a very different place. Homeless men and women inhabited the underbelly where the abutments marked the beginning and end of the structure. Tonight, though, everything appeared quiet. That didn't stop the nervousness in her stomach at the way the lights made shadows on the ground. Her hands shook with fear, even though she tried to portray a sense of calm. Looking at her watch, she cursed. Her contact was almost an hour late, and she was about to jump out of her skin.

"I'm gonna wait five more minutes, and if the asshole isn't here by then I'm leaving," she muttered.

Tyler had tried calling her on her way here, but she'd ignored the call. She was sick of all of this. Denise had been right, she was a pawn and she didn't know how to make this better. Maybe Tyler could help her, maybe he couldn't.

Blowing out a deep breath, she turned to begin her pacing again. Out of nowhere, something hard hit her from behind, and she fell to the ground face first. Stunned, she tried to rise up on her elbows, only to feel the hardness of a male body atop hers. She tried to scream, but a gloved hand clamped over her mouth. Thinking quickly, she launched her teeth into the skin of the leather, but it did nothing more than muffle her scream even further. Thrashing about, she threw her head back trying to hit her attacker, but the assailant grabbed her hair tightly and pulled. Tears sprang to her eyes as she tried to escape, screaming hoarsely. Releasing his hand from her mouth, he shoved her face in the dirt, rocks, and trash that littered the ground.

"Please," she begged, feeling his hand skim her backside as he pulled her pants and underwear from her body. "No," she cried into the ground.

At this moment, she knew that no one could hear her. Trying to scream only succeeded in more dirt coating her tongue and throat. She dug her fingers into the ground, feeling her nails break as she clawed at the dirt.

"This is a message, and I hope you hear it loud and clear bitch. Stop tryin' to play clubs against each other."

All too soon, she could feel his nakedness against her skin and then he shoved himself into her from behind. She cried out, trying desperately to get as far away from the pain as she could. It lasted for only minutes, but felt like hours. She prayed harder than she'd ever prayed that this man would be fast. The feel of semen hitting her back repulsed her so much that she vomited.

The man turned her over, and she fought to look at him, notice anything about him that may help her later. She squinted up at him, but he wore a black mask and there was no light. She did see blue eyes so she knew he was Caucasian.

"You keep your nose out of club business or even worse will happen to you next time," he threatened.

She could do nothing more than nod as tears streamed down her face. He began to get up, but as he did he leaned over her, and his fist knocked her first to the left and then to the right. She curled up into a ball, trying to protect herself as he hit her again and again. When he was finished, he pulled a dollar bill from his pocket and threw it down on her chest.

"For services rendered."

As he walked away, she heard his phone ring with a ringtone that would forever be implanted into her brain. A little girl sang *Happy Birthday dear daddy*. This man was someone's father; the thought made her even sicker.

She waited a full five minutes before raising herself to her knees and pulling her pants up. Her body screamed in pain, and she groaned loudly. Swaying, she wiped the blood from her face and looked around slowly. Her vision swam as she fought to drag herself up to where she had parked her car. There were no steps to take her to the parking lot, and her body protested in agony with every step she took. It had been through a lot the past few days. Just as she crested the top of the hill and pulled herself up, she heard the rumbling of a bike echo through the night.

Shivering, despite the fact that she now sweated, she pulled her tattered shirt tightly around her body, keeping her head down. She had no idea where her jacket had gone, and she hadn't thought to look for it. Meredith didn't know if this bike was friend or foe and, to be honest, she had few friends when it came to the biker community. That was now painfully true. The bike pulled in next to her car, and it took all the courage she possessed to look at the rider. Her lips trembling, her teeth chattering, she cried out when she saw that it was Tyler.

"Help me," she whispered, her lip quivering as the tears and shakes overtook her body.

"Good God, Meredith. I've been looking for you everywhere. What the hell happened?" he asked as he took his helmet off and strode quickly over to meet her.

"Take me home," she pleaded.

Taking in the bruising high on her cheekbones, around her eyes, and the blood caking her lips, he shook his head. "Home, hell. You need a doctor."

"No doctor! Just take me home."

He cursed, he had been too late in warning her. He'd gone to her duplex and waited for hours. When she hadn't shown up, he'd taken off, searching the city for her car. Finally seeing it sitting in this empty parking lot had struck him in the solar plexus. Pulling out his pre-pay, he punched in a familiar number.

"Yeah, I found her, but she's been beaten badly. If you aren't home, you go check on Denise right now. I have a feelin' this is just the beginning."

He hung up and held his hand out to her. "Give me your keys. I'm taking you someplace safe."

Meredith wanted to argue with him, tell him that she didn't need to be taken anywhere besides home. Instead she handed him the keys she'd had in her pocket the whole time. Listlessly laying them in his palm, she sobbed.

"Why didn't I use those? I had them in my pocket. Why didn't I use it to stab his fucking eyes out?"

Tyler didn't know what to do. If he tried to put his arms around her, would she flinch? Did she need comfort?

"You did the best you could with what you had, and that's all anybody can ask."

His calm words washed over her, and he directed her to the passenger side of her car. Once he had her in, he made another call on his cell. In the distance she could hear him asking a Prospect to come and get his bike. When he got in behind the wheel, she knew they were heading for the clubhouse, and she had to wonder exactly what kind of reception would be waiting her there.

Chapter Twenty-Five

D enise sighed deeply; it had been a very long day. She and Mandy had decided to completely clean the house they had been calling home, and her body was screaming. It was obvious to her she needed to start a workout program once her body allowed her to actually bend her arms after this. Of course Mandy hadn't felt anything, she'd run off with Andrew as soon as the sun had gone down. They had started having bonfires at night with other club kids and some of the younger club members. It had bothered her at first, but now she realized just how much she enjoyed her peaceful nights. She also loved that her kids had met others who lived this life and who understood it. The development of her kids was *the* most important thing to her, and in the past few days she realized just how much of a home *they* had made here. Their independence gave her independence, and that was a great gift that she had not counted on when she started this.

"Oh shower, how I love you," she moaned, letting the hot water rush over her sore muscles. Just maybe she'd be able to walk in the morning. If she played her cards right. When her fingers were pruned and the water began running cool, she got out. The hot water heater in this house was huge, so if she'd used it all, she had been in there quite a while.

Shutting the water off and stepping out, she winced as she reached over to grab her towel. The muscles in her back protested, and she groaned. Wrapping the towel around her body, she grabbed her brush and tried to pull it through hair made curly by the shower. The steam in the bathroom at least made her muscles feel pliant, and she felt like she could move just a little bit better.

"I am in such bad shape," she groaned. This must be how most women felt after doing Zumba for the first time.

Carefully walking into the bedroom, she sat on the bed and unwrapped the towel from her body. Downstairs, she could hear the front door shut and smiled, it was about time Liam got home.

"Liam, I need a massage," she yelled, leaning back on the bed and striking a pose. She had never done anything like that, but maybe it was time she started. Denise hoped that he would appreciate it.

She waited for a few minutes, and when there was no answer she called out again. "Liam?"

The stairs creaked, but she noticed that she hadn't heard the heavy stomping of his motorcycle boots. There had been no noise of him putting his keys on the table in the hallway, she hadn't heard the shuffling of mail that he usually brought in. Something wasn't right. The hairs on her arms stood on end, and she began to feel uneasy. Her aching body protested as she quickly sat up, grabbing sweats and a shirt that Liam had left beside the bed after his workout earlier in the day. They swallowed her whole, and she cursed as she tried desperately to tie the drawstring on the pants. The bottom of the pants went well over the edges of her feet, and she fought to kick them out of her way. Her hands shook violently, but she finally got them tied and tiptoed her way back into the bathroom. She closed the door and locked it before sinking down in between the toilet and the wall. If anything happened, maybe it would offer her some sort of protection.

Her heart beat rapidly, threatening to come out of her chest. She felt like one of those crazy girls in a horror movie waiting to die. Trying to regulate the breath rushing out of her mouth, she heard the floor creak in the bedroom and slapped her hand over her mouth to keep herself from screaming. She wished she had something, anything, to protect herself with. The door handle jiggled as someone tried to turn it. Moments passed and she thought that maybe the person on the other side of the door had left. She was just about to get up when muffled gunshots sounded and bullets came through the door near the door knob. It felt like time was moving in slow motion. She could swear she saw the bullets whizzing by with her eyes.

That was it; she screamed bloody murder and cursed herself for backing into a corner. Now she had nowhere to go. A glass jar sat on the counter, holding q-tips. Thinking quickly, she grabbed it, throwing it as the door opened. Sheer luck finally won out as it hit the intruder in the head, and he screamed, blood pouring out of the knit mask that covered his face. He was tall and she was willing to bet he was strongly built. He took up most of the doorway that he stood in. If he approached her for hand-to-hand combat, he would likely kill her, and she knew that she couldn't allow that to happen.

Downstairs, the front door crashed open, and Denise heard Liam's voice yelling for her.

"Upstairs. There's a guy with a gun!" She screamed, hoping with everything that she had that Liam could save her.

The man in the doorway glared at her. The only thing visible were blue eyes, and it looked like he was contemplating what he wanted to do with her. They both could hear Liam scrambling up the stairs, and the guy with the gun made a split decision. He turned, aiming the gun at the window in the bedroom, and shot it out, jumping from the second story just as Liam made it into the doorway. Liam held his own gun and yelled as the unknown man jumped from his bedroom window.

"You okay?" he asked Denise as he saw her standing in the bathroom, her face pale and her body shaking.

"Yeah, thanks to you. I hit him in the head, he probably can't make it far," she informed him, motioning to all the glass on the floor.

"That's my girl." He pulled out his cell, letting the person on the other end know that Denise was fine and what had happened. Hanging up, he motioned toward her.

"Did he hurt you?"

Shaking her head, she answered. "No, I hid in the bathroom, like a wuss."

"Nothing wrong with stayin' alive, baby." He crossed the threshold and scooped her up in his arms.

Hugging herself tightly to his body, she buried her head in his shoulder and let him know what her worst thoughts had been. "I really thought I was a goner there for a minute. I thought it was you at first, and I was lying naked on the bed."

He shuddered, knowing just what could have happened. Knowing the horrors that had been done to Meredith, he breathed easier. "Thank God you figured out it wasn't. Pack some stuff. We're goin' on lockdown at the clubhouse. They hit Meredith tonight too."

Her blood ran cold. Something felt off. "What do you mean they hit her?"

Framing her face with his hands, he told her the news he didn't want to tell. But he knew that he had to be honest with her. "She was beaten and raped. Tyler found her and brought her to the clubhouse. Right now she needs her friend. Can you pack some clothes for her?"

Was that what the man had been planning to do to her? Was this a planned attack on the club? "Was he going to do that to me?" she asked, eyes wide.

"I don't know, but at this point we have to assume the worst. That's why we're going on lockdown. Even my damn mother will be there," he grumbled.

She knew there was danger if his mother was going to be included in the protected bunch. "Let me get a bag. Are the kids already there?"

"They are," he confirmed. "You want me to pack for us while you pack for them?"

"We're just all gonna sleep out in the open?" she asked, wondering what kind of clothes she should pack. Her hands shook with the residual adrenaline that coursed through her body. She dropped her bag twice before she finally picked it up and took a deep breath.

"No darlin'. Brothers have dorm rooms," he put his hands on her shoulders, calming her with his mere presence. He knew that what had transpired had affected her.

She didn't know what that meant, but she assumed this was another lesson in the world of a motorcycle club.

They arrived a few hours later, having boarded up the house as best as they could. The gate that usually stood open at the edge of the clubhouse's property was only standing part way open. She recognized Prospects and lesser members of the club standing guard. Men stood on the roof of the clubhouse, watching over the groups of people coming in. They held guns, and it felt like she had stepped into a war zone.

"Grab your stuff and let's get inside." Liam's tone of voice said there would be no argument. They needed to get inside where it was safe. He didn't mind being out in the open, but he most definitely didn't want her out there.

Tyler met him as Liam got out of his truck. "You're the last of them," Tyler informed them.

Liam turned back to where the Prospects and members stood at the gate. "Lock it down."

He watched with keen eyes as the gate was closed and locked. Parking rollbacks and wreckers in front of it provided an extra barrier of protection. Reaching over, he grabbed one of the bags that Denise carried and ushered her into the clubhouse.

As they walked in, her breath hitched. There looked to be a couple hundred people there. She hadn't realized how large the clubhouse was. She greeted the few people she knew and stuck close to Liam. Feeling her unease, he wrapped an arm around her neck, pulling her in front of his body and letting her rest against him.

"You're fine here," he reassured her.

"I know, I'm just kinda put off by all the people." Even as confident as she had grown, insecurities still lay just below the surface. She wondered how many of these women Liam had slept with.

"It's okay, it's a lot to take in." He tried to see this through her eyes. Walking into this place with all these people that she didn't know had to be intimidating.

William got everyone's attention as he stood at the front of the room. "I want to welcome everyone and let you know that while you're here, you're safe. We have a threat to this club and everyone involved with us. While we have some business to take care of, you will all remain here. Any concerns, you see one of us and we'll do our best to help you. We're at full capacity so please have some patience with one another. Enjoy your stay."

Liam leaned against the back wall, keeping his arm around her. "Do you need anything?" he asked.

"Just need to know where to put our stuff."

"Let me take you to my dorm," he bent down, grabbing one of the duffels they had brought with them.

They weaved their way through the large group that had gathered. He kept her hand in his, looking anyone in the eye who watched them. With this many men and women around, he wanted to let them know she was his and he was hers. It wouldn't do for everyone to be fighting or to cause a fight because feelings weren't clear. As they got to the hallway that led to the dorms, an older woman stepped in front of them.

"Liam, it's good to see you."

Denise felt his body tense, so she wrapped a comforting hand around his forearm. She wondered who this was, and it was on the tip of her tongue to ask. Instead, Liam took a physical step back and schooled his face to be completely devoid of any emotion.

"Lauren, wish I could say the same."

Lauren. This was his mother, the one he never spoke about. She was standing right here in front of them. Denise wondered if there would be an introduction.

"Is this the woman in your life son? Aren't you going to introduce us?"

Sighing deeply, he side stepped her. "I'd really rather not."

With that, he pulled Denise down the hallway until they reached a room with his name on it. Pulling keys out of his pocket, he unlocked the door and shoved her inside. Anger radiated off his body as he pushed her against the now closed door and planted a kiss on her lips.

The predatory look in his eyes made her hot and scared her all at the same time. "Finally, we're alone at last."

Chapter Twenty-Six

"As alone as we can be with a clubhouse full of people around," she quipped.

"I wish we were completely alone. Just you, me, and the kids. I don't want all this other stuff, I don't need it right now. It just stresses me out," he admitted. His eyes were jumpy and darted back and forth between her and the door.

Understanding dawned on her when she realized this was his coping mechanism. He wanted to bury himself in her life to escape from his. Not deal with his Mom or any of the drama that whole situation brought. She had to get his mind on something else. Sex would never be the answer to any of their problems. "Besides, before we get some alone time I need to check on my kids, and I want to check on Meredith."

He groaned, knowing that she was right. They each had responsibilities, and it wouldn't do to just throw them to the wayside. After seeing his mother, he felt vulnerable. He hadn't been prepared to see her that soon, hadn't expected the anger that came so quickly. In retrospect he should have. He always seemed to see red where she was concerned, but he wished just once he felt some other type of emotion. He hated that was all that Denise saw when it came to him and the woman that birthed him. Denise was his strength and calming factor. Sighing, he ran his hands down her arms and clasped her hands. "I know. I'm sure there's work I could be doing too, but doing you would be so much more fun."

She giggled as she opened the door to the dorm room and then walked out. The look she threw back his way told him that she felt the same way.

"Do you have any idea where you're going?" he asked as he saw her stop and look both ways down the hall trying to figure out where she needed to go. Instead of asking, she turned back to him, held her hands up, and shook her head. "You're so cute," he told her, putting his hands on her hips.

She blushed. "You got me. I have absolutely no idea where I'm going. Can you show me where everyone is?"

He took her hand and directed them down the hallway. She loved walking with his hand in hers. She had never noticed it before, but he walked around like he owned the place. There was such an air about him, such a swagger of authority. Like he dared someone to come up to him and try to assert themselves over him. It was heady and she loved it. He made her feel protected at all times. Even now when she knew he was vulnerable with his kryptonite in the house. She had not one ounce of fear. She didn't have any doubts – he could handle anything that anyone handed him.

"The kids will be in here," he indicated a door with their clasped hands. "This is where the kids usually sleep when we have lockdowns."

"Is a lockdown a normal part of life in the club?" She was genuinely curious.

"Would that change how you feel about this whole situation?" Liam hoped not. He liked their situation just as it was but knew she wanted a stable environment for her kids – and he did not begrudge her that.

She tilted her head and pulled her bottom lip between her teeth. "I don't think so. I mean I've already been shot at. My house was vandalized, and I've already broken the law for you. I think it's safe to say I'm already in pretty deep. I'm not goin' anywhere," she surprised him by winking.

Liam grinned, putting his hands around her waist and pulling her body so that they were flush with one another. He dropped his head and kissed her softly before pulling back and giving her the killer smile he seemed to reserve only for her. "I'm glad to know that. To answer your question we've only had about three lockdowns that I can remember since my dad founded this club. It's violent, don't get me wrong, but it's usually not this bad."

She cracked open the door, peeking in on her kids. She saw bunk beds taking up the walls, separated into boys and girls sides. All children appeared to be co-habitating well. She saw Mandy sitting at a laptop with another girl whose name she remembered was Layla. The two of them had taken to one another pretty quickly, and she had heard the name mentioned more than once. Drew sat at a table playing a card game with a group of boys. Feeling secure about where they were, she waved her fingers at her kids and turned back to him.

Now that she knew they were okay, she could concentrate on her friend. "Where's Meredith?"

He grabbed her hand again, leading her into a room that had Tyler's name on it. That took her by surprise, but she had known the Sergeant-at-Arms would be watching over her friend in some way. "She's staying with Tyler?"

Shrugging, he knocked quietly on the door. "He found her, and he refuses to leave her side. When it comes to him, none of us really ask any questions. If he wants us to know something, he's usually very forthcoming."

They waited a few moments for someone to come answer the door. When Tyler finally appeared, he stepped out and closed the door so that the three of them were alone in the hallway. "She's been asking for you," he motioned to Denise.

"Should I know anything before I see her?"

His eyes were shadowed, displaying more emotion than Denise had ever seen from the normally quiet man. Obviously Meredith was in a bad way, and he was trying hard to keep it together. "I'm trying to convince her to either go get checked out or let me call the club doc. She's in bad shape. I haven't let her go take a shower yet. Try to talk her into letting someone come take care of her. Maybe since you're a woman, you can appeal to her sensible side."

She nodded. He wasn't asking her, he was telling her. "I'll do what I can."

He smiled grimly, his lips making a thin line before stepping aside, letting her open the door. When she walked in and shut it quietly, Liam placed his hand on Tyler's shoulder and squeezed.

"We'll find out who did this brother."

Tyler nodded. "Yeah, and I'll kill the motherfucker with my bare hands." The quiet spoken words were not a promise, they were a vow.

Denise walked in, noting that only one light was turned on and it was over on the far side of the room. Meredith lay with her back facing the door, curled into the fetal position. Not wanting to scare the other woman, Denise cleared her throat and walked over so that they were facing each other.

"Holy mother of God," she whispered, getting her first glimpse of the devastation that had been dealt to Meredith's face.

"It's bad isn't it?" Meredith asked, tears making her throat tight. It hurt to push the words out. She wasn't sure if it was from where he'd shoved her face in the ground or where she had spent so much time screaming. All she knew was that she could still feel blood seeping from some of the wounds.

"I won't lie to you, it is. You really need to see a doctor."

Going to the bathroom that sat just off the room, Denise grabbed a washcloth and ran cold water over it. This gave her a little bit of time to compose herself. No matter how Tyler had tried to warn her, she couldn't believe how bad Meredith's face was. She folded the washcloth up in her hand and made her way back to the bed. Kneeling down, she began to clean the dried blood off of the tiny cuts marring the usually perfect skin. Tears pooled in her eyes as she gently ran the washcloth over her face. It broke her heart as tears slipped from Meredith's eye lids, running down the dirt caked on her cheeks.

"I can't believe I let this happen," she whispered, a sob shaking her body.

Denise cautiously got on the bed, motioning for Meredith to sit up. Gingerly, she put her arm around the other woman, providing her as much comfort as she was allowed to. "You don't *let* something like this happen. An evil person does this to another."

"I fought him," she choked out, sobs erupting from her chest and wracking her shoulders.

"I bet you did," Denise whispered. She couldn't help the tears that came to her eyes. This was her friend, and she almost didn't recognize her. It was the most horrible thing she had ever seen in her life.

Meredith held her hands out in front of her, and Denise saw the fingernails, most of them broken to the quick, stained with blood and dirt. There was evidence here, and it needed to be catalogued.

"I'm telling you this woman to woman. If I was in your situation, I'd see a doctor. There's no shame in getting the person who did this to you." She wanted so badly to shake her friend, to make her see that not getting checked out might as well be a death sentence. There was no telling what kind of damage had been done, not only externally, but internally as well – who knew what kind of diseases this man possibly carried.

"I feel like I asked for it," she admitted, clearing her throat as it clogged with more emotion.

"Why? You were just doing a job."

Meredith ran a shaky hand through her hair. "They *all* warned me off. Hell, Tyler told me if I went through with this he'd never be able to protect me. What did I do though? I kept at it. I kept pressing my luck. I asked for this."

"Nobody asks for this. Nobody." Denise had to make her see, make her agree to let the doctor come in. It was obvious that she did need medical help.

Reaching into her pants pocket, Meredith pulled out a dollar bill. "He threw this on me when he was done. He said it was for *services rendered.*"

Denise saw red. In that moment, she understood why others murdered. She understood the blind rage that made someone want to avenge a loved one. "You believe that and you're a fool. You are a strong woman; you don't let shit like this get you down. Allow a doctor to come here and nail this asshole to the wall, Meredith. Don't let him do this to someone else."

She shook her head. "I just don't think I can."

Trying another method, Denise tried to keep her tone calm. "If it was me or Mandy, what would you say?"

A grim determination finally formed in Meredith's eyes and she set her jaw. "I'd tell you to fry the motherfucker."

"Then what makes you any different? Let's get him. If we can find out who he is, we can make sure he spends the rest of his life trying to get it up and not being able to."

"What if the club kills him? That's blood on my hands," Meredith had no doubt that Tyler would gladly rip the man from limb to limb. He had all but said so in the time he had spent with her since this had all gone down.

Eyes glittering, Denise shook her head vehemently. "No, not at all. That's a justified killing."

Meredith saw the change come over the other woman, it was almost like she was seeing her for the first time. When they met, Denise had been mousy, so cut down by life. Now she was ready to kill to avenge another person's honor. And not just any person. Hers. Someone who had tried to warn her off of all the changes she was making. Someone who was trying to protect her, only to end up getting hurt in the process. It was scary and amazing all at the same time.

"I don't want anybody doing anything stupid. Especially you and Tyler, but I will consent to seeing a doctor. My ribs are killing me."

If that's what she wanted, then Denise would make it happen. "Let me go tell Tyler. We'll get a doctor here as soon as possible."

When Denise left, Meredith lay back down on the bed, her head spinning. She prayed she had made the right decision.

Chapter Twenty-Seven

Meredith closed her eyes as the doctor performed a rape kit on her. She tried to transport herself to a time where she felt safe and secure. She realized it'd been a long time since she had felt that way for any long stretch, but it surprised her to realize she'd felt that way with Tyler every time they had been around one another.

The doctor raised her head from between Meredith's spread thighs and snapped her gloves off. Straightening up, she grabbed a digital camera. "I'm done, Meredith. Now let me get some pictures of your injuries."

It was obvious she was trying to be careful with her patient, but Meredith still felt as if she were on display. She tried not to wonder where this woman had gotten her MD, and it bothered her a bit that Tyler had greeted the woman with a hug. He didn't greet people with hugs, and it had struck her as odd. The look that had passed between him and Ashley, the doctor, had made her inexplicably jealous. It spoke of nights spent together and secret liaisons. She didn't like it one bit.

"Do you want me to let Tyler back in?" she asked as she powered down the camera and tucked it away in her bag.

Shaking her head, she mumbled. "No, I'd rather just get this over with if it's okay?"

Ten minutes later she was putting her clothes back on and waiting for the doctor to tell her what to do.

"Now, you can go take a shower. I'm going to leave some antibiotics and the morning-after pill with Tyler. I'll also give him some pain pills and a few sleeping pills. Complete the round of antibiotics and take everything I'm giving you. I know you said he didn't finish inside you, but you can't ever be too cautious."

Those words caused Meredith to shake. Pregnancy thanks to a rape. That would just be her luck. Or some disease there was no cure for. She had always been very discriminate with the men she slept with, almost to the point of being labeled a prude at times. Now she had this to deal with?

"I warn you to be careful with the pain and sleeping pills. If you need more, you will need to come see me again. Monitoring you closely will prevent you from developing a dependency on them. I do recommend that you take the sleeping pill, at least for a couple of days. Your body needs rest to heal, and you have a lot of healing to do. If you need the name of a counselor, I can recommend someone to you."

Meredith knew the woman was doing her job, but she just wanted her to leave. This was all too much for her. It was too much information too fast. She wanted desperately to take the blanket from the bed and cocoon herself in it, shutting out the rest of the world for days. What had started out as a beautiful day when she had woken up that morning had turned into a complete nightmare. One that she wanted to wake up from but didn't know if she ever would.

"I don't think I'll be needing that right now." Her voice didn't even sound like her own to her ears. It sounded like a different person was talking. The last thing she wanted to do was spill her guts to some stranger. It would be horrible, explaining to them what that man had done to her. Telling Denise the one small detail she had was more painful than she had imagined. No way could she tell a stranger the entire story.

Ashley gave a small nod of acceptance. Not everyone was open to therapy, especially so soon after the attack, but it was still her job to let a patient know all of the available options. It would be up to the patient which option, if any, they decided to take. "I'll leave all the information with Tyler. If you do need it in the future, at least you'll have it. Is that okay?"

Meredith nodded, her mind racing a million miles a minute. How was she supposed to feel? What was she supposed to say? She wasn't sure, and it felt like she should have at least a few of those answers – but she didn't and she wondered if she ever would.

"Do you have any questions for me?" Ashley asked softly, carefully, almost like you would approach an animal that had been hurt.

"No, I just want to be left alone," Meredith shook her head. She could taste it, the solitude she craved so desperately.

Ashley smiled sadly at her. "That's not unusual, but please try not to isolate. I'll leave you to take a shower.

You'll probably feel much better. Be sure and put Neosporin on those fingernails. Do you need some?"

She shook her head, her eyes glazing over. *Just leave me alone.* She wanted to shout. "No, Tyler has a first aid kit. I'm sure there's some in there."

"Then I'll leave you alone. Remember if you need anything, call me."

"Or have Tyler call you, right?" Meredith didn't know why she was being so snarky, but this doctor really just hit her the wrong way.

Ashley couldn't help her grin. Any little bit of spirit within this woman boded well for her future. "You're very observant."

"I'm a reporter." Even that sounded like it came from a little kid who hadn't gotten her way. It was filled with venom and brattiness.

"Tyler was my rebellion as a teenager. We've stayed friends. It's not like that with us. There's a lot of respect. It's not like I wear his tattoo or his patch," Ashley explained.

Meredith didn't exactly know what that meant, but it made her happy. Dismissing the good doc, she went to the bathroom and closed the door.

Once inside, Meredith engaged the lock and turned around pressing her back against the door, sliding until she hit the ground. She was in shock, she supposed, not able to believe that this was in fact happening to her – had happened to her. She still hadn't seen what she looked like. Tyler had kept her away from mirrors, and it scared her to know what she hadn't seen. Would she be able to stomach what she saw? That ran through her mind. What if she didn't look like herself anymore? Forcing her sore muscles to support her, she walked over to the bathroom mirror and gasped.

Her eye was swollen shut on one side – which she had figured, she was having trouble seeing but had made herself believe it was the low light in the bedroom. Her lips were cracked, there were scratches all over her face. Her nails that had been her pride and joy at the news station were completely wrecked. The manicure she had given herself a few days before – all nails a dark gray except for her ring nail a bright pink – was gone. It had made her smile every time she had looked down at it. Now the nail polish was chipped, in some cases no longer even there. For some reason, that depressed her more than anything. That was the straw that broke the proverbial camel's back.

Turning the water on, she tried to squelch the tears that had begun spilling over her lashes. Steam rose in the bathroom and she reached for the cell phone she'd brought in with her. Sending a text to her manager, she asked for a leave of absence before getting into the shower. Letting the warm water wash over her body, she broke down again.

When Ashley shut the dorm room door behind her, she was met with three sets of anxious eyes. Holding up her hands, she warded off their questions.

"She's fragile, barely holding it together, just like Denise told me before I went in there. You guys have *got* to be careful with her," she warned, looking squarely and directly at Tyler. There was no way he knew just how close Meredith was to the edge, just how little it would take to push her over.

"Did she tell you anything?" Tyler asked.

If she hadn't known him for as long as she had, she would be completely terrified. He made such an imposing figure, leaning against the wall, huge arms crossed over his chest. Dark eyes so serious, staring holes into her. Ashley, however, knew how to deal with him and refused to be intimidated.

"No, she's very quiet about it. That's kind of what worries me. I'm leaving you some sleeping and pain pills for her. You watch her with them. I don't think she's suicidal, but you never know how people are after something like this. That's always a concern. If she spikes a fever or gets worse through the night, call me. I also suspect she has a mild concussion. Wake her up throughout the night and make sure she can answer a few simple questions. She should be able to, even on this medication. Anything strikes you as weird, call me, I mean it," she stabbed Tyler with a look that dared him to ignore her.

They all nodded, and she handed the bag of pill bottles to Tyler. "In addition, make sure she takes every antibiotic in that bag. It will protect her from STD's and any other virus the man may have been carrying. There's also the morning-after pill in there, she needs to take it immediately after she takes a shower. I've also got her on a round of HIV medication. You called me in enough time that everything should be okay, but it's imperative that she follow these recommendations. I told her all of this, but she wasn't too impressed with me. I want you to reiterate."

Tyler nodded. These were all things he hadn't been in the right mind to think of. This was why he was glad he had called Ashley, because all of this was scaring the absolute shit out of him. "I'll make sure she takes everything."

She knew that he would.

"Everything she should take tonight, I have in that little container," she indicated a clear pill bottle. "The rest, you should be able to figure out. Like I said, questions, call."

"We got it."

She grabbed all her stuff and turned to leave. Before she made it all the way out the door, she turned. "Be patient with her and try not to force her. Have her come to you. Denise, you talked her into seeing me, try to talk her into seeing a therapist. I have a feeling she's going to need it."

The officers sat around their conference table discussing club business.

"What are we going to do about Richard?" Liam asked, looking at all of the men he called 'brother'.

"Well, we can't just wait on him, we could be here forever."

William turned to communications expert Steele. "Can we figure out where he stays?"

"It shouldn't take too long. I hacked into his bank accounts the other day, and he's paying AT&T so my money's on the fact that he's got an iPhone. That's got a GPS on it."

Liam grinned. "There's an app for that."

"That there is." Steele grinned back. "There is one good thing about the technological boom. It makes my job easier."

"Okay," William boomed. "You find out where he is. We need to watch him a couple of days and get his pattern. We've got everybody on lockdown here, so we should be able to do it relatively easy. We get his pattern, and then we strike when he least expects it."

Tyler cleared his throat. "If we find out for sure he's behind Meredith's rape, I want him."

"I understand that, but this is club business," William started.

"That wasn't a request, Pres.," Tyler interrupted.

Normally the president of the club wouldn't deal with someone interrupting him and making demands, but Tyler was different. To put it mildly, pretty much everyone was just a little bit scared of the Native American with the wild look in his eyes.

"Duly noted."

"So what do we do now?"

Liam answered. "Now boys, we just sit back and wait. He's gonna hang himself, we just have to give him enough rope."

Chapter Twenty-Eight

Richard Joyce knew he had to do something. Bookies were *this close* to putting out hits on him, but one in particular was willing to deal. He wanted a piece of property located on Highway 185 that belonged to the club. If he could get his hands on that land, he knew he would be able to wipe his slate clean and perhaps live another year. A plan had developed in his head. He could give the bookie a small piece of the land and then take the rest to sell for a profit. The overage would allow him to set up residence elsewhere *and* stay alive. He had to get this taken care of and the sooner the better. The bank would know sooner rather than later that he'd begun to skim off the top. Prominent citizens of Bowling Green were bound to start noticing their bank accounts becoming smaller. Amounts taken out weren't exorbitant, but Richard knew that many of them kept a close watch on their accounts. His game was about to be up, and he knew it. Something had to happen, and it had to be now. When this started, he only thought it would be for a short while, he couldn't keep this up.

Not for the first time he cursed his gambling habit. Something he had never been able to give up. Even with the club it had been bad – so bad that he probably still owed them dues – because he'd never been able to afford them when they were owed. He figured he had never learned one good lesson in his life, and this was probably how it was supposed to end up.

At his side, his phone rang and he answered, not sure of the number. It seemed like he was getting calls at all hours of the day from unknown numbers. It did no good to screen them, they just kept calling. He sighed as he answered.

"Yeah?"

"The reporter is taken care of. She won't be a problem after today." The voice was low, sounding like a movie villain.

Richard's eyebrows drew together in question, and his stomach dropped. Whatever *this* was, wasn't good. "Who are you, and what the hell are you talking about? I never ordered a hit on a reporter."

The voice on the other end of the phone caused goose bumps to break out over his arms and neck. This did not feel good.

"You did, and I want the other half of my payment." The steel of the voice told Richard not to argue, but he wouldn't be blamed for something he damn well didn't do.

"I don't know who the fuck you are. I'm not sure how to explain that to you any more clearly than I already have," Richard argued.

"Well then we have a bit of a problem, Richard Joyce, because I know *everything* about you. I did a job in your name and was paid half for it up front, and now I want my other half. I want that money by the end of business tomorrow."

The dial tone in his ear was the only thing that told him the phone call was over.

Richard cursed loudly. Someone had set him up and now he had two people gunning for him. He slammed the phone down and ran a hand through his hair. It was time to either pull the plug on himself or pull the trigger on his plan – whichever he decided it had to be done now. Either way, he figured this was the end and he'd be dead soon anyhow.

Steele sat in front of the bank of monitors that watched the numerous interests the club had around the city and beyond. They were almost certain that Richard was going to hit one of them, they just weren't sure which. He stretched lazily. It felt like he'd been sitting there forever.

"Everything good?" Liam asked as he took a seat next to the other man.

"Everything's quiet. Too quiet really. I expect something to happen very soon. It hasn't *ever* been this quiet. Spooky quiet."

Just as he said that, a group of men appeared on one of the screens. They wore all black. From hooded sweatshirts to black pants, gloves, and boots. The two of them watched as they broke into a warehouse and breached the front door.

"This is it. Get everybody ready, it's time to move."

Chaos erupted inside the clubhouse as everyone went about the jobs they had been assigned. The tension was thick as the women and a few Prospects watched the patched members leave. Everyone all hoped for the same thing, that the men would come back intact and no one else would get hurt.

Hours later, Denise walked out the back door of the clubhouse where a concrete porch had been poured. Sitting down on a lounge chair, she sighed. The tension in the clubhouse was too much for her to deal with any longer. In order to breathe, she felt that she needed to be somewhere else. Somewhere she could let her shoulders drop and lungs expand.

"This is the part that sucks, huh?" She looked up as Roni came to sit next to her.

Denise chuckled dryly, running a hand through her hair. "Yeah, I've never been very patient anyway. I'm not used to wondering if this violence will touch my family or not. It unnerves me a little bit."

Roni could understand how someone who hadn't been brought up in the lifestyle could be worried or confused. She chose to believe that everyone would come back unscathed. They always had. It was the only way she could get through it herself.

"I've never wondered if someone wouldn't come home. How weird is that? I've always believed Dad and Liam can handle themselves. Does that make me odd?"

Denise laughed. "Not at all. I wish I could be like that. I've never been the type of person that just let life be. I always want control of it. I'm scared of the unknown —

always have been. I guess that's what happens when you get pregnant with twins as a teenager."

She watched as her friend looked back into the clubhouse where her mom sat on a couch by herself. It was obvious from the look in her eyes that she wanted to go sit next to Lauren, offer her comfort of some sort. Possibly work on their relationship in a way that Liam didn't want to do.

"You don't have to babysit me, ya know? Why don't you go spend some time with your mom while the guys aren't here? You can do it with no animosity or looks of death from Liam."

Roni smiled. "Maybe you can soften him up. But until then, I think I'm gonna take you up on that."

Denise watched as the other woman went into the house and again sighed. She was keyed up and unnerved. She didn't want her kids or anyone else to see it, but she was feeling wild with nerves. Walking to the edge of the porch, she wrapped her arms around her body. It was a warm night, but there was a chill she felt from somewhere else. She looked up at the night sky, amazed again by how much she could see out here in the middle of nowhere. Knowing that Liam could look up and see the same sky calmed her a little. When she tilted her head back, a fist wrapped in her hair and pulled it sharply. She made the motion to scream, but a gloved hand went over her open mouth. She inhaled, a sweet smell making its way into her nostrils, lethargy immediately claimed her body and she went limp.

"Can't believe the VP left you out here with no protection. Denise Cunningham, you're coming with me."

Later, members of the club arrived back at the clubhouse, all pissed.

"Is it over?" Roni asked, hope in her voice.

"Not even close. It apparently hasn't even started. When we got there, no one was there. The lock wasn't even broken. I saw that damn lock break on the video. I don't like the feel of this," Liam grunted, getting off the bike.

He strode through the clubhouse, frustration apparent in every step he took. This man was playing with them all, and he couldn't expect for it to continue.

"Where's Denise?" he asked Roni. He wanted to bury his feelings in his woman for an hour or two. She took away the tension he always seemed to feel.

"She was out back on the porch when I last saw her. Mom and I have been talking for a while."

Panic seized him and cold seeped into his muscles. "You left her out there by herself?"

"Yeah, she's a big girl and we *are* safe here, remember?" She didn't like his tone, didn't appreciate the implications of it.

"Safe is a motherfucking relative term with this asshole. You better hope she's still out there."

Dread curled up in Roni's stomach. For some reason she felt scared, and her breath came in short gasps. She watched as Liam went out to the back porch and then turned around, ice in his eyes.

"She's not out there, Roni. Where the fuck is she? How long have you been in here?"

Roni tried desperately to remember what time she had come back inside the building. The conversation with Lauren had been exactly what she needed and time had flown by. "A few hours maybe?"

"You don't know where she's been for a few hours? After I deal with him, I'm gonna deal with you. Sister or not. Let me guess, *you* probably had something to do with it," he pointed his eyes towards Lauren. "I'm sure you'd pay off anyone who wanted to hurt me."

"No," Lauren shook her head, but he cut her off with a glare.

For the first time in her life, Roni was scared of her brother. She saw the murderous rage in his eyes and the look that made other men cower. Roni tried to pull him into her arms, just like she had a million times before, but he shrugged her off and went in search of William. He saw Steele on the way and shouted.

"Track that motherfucker's cell phone right now. He's got Denise."

His brothers had heard him shouting, they had heard the fear and panic in his voice. Everyone had come running. In the corner of his eye, he could see Mandy and Drew. For the first time in his life, his mother did something that helped him. She herded them back into the kids' area. It wasn't quick enough for him not to see Drew's eyes. The disappointment in those eyes killed him. He always swore when he'd had his own children that he'd never see that in their eyes. He'd be damned if it happened now. Walking over to that room, he motioned for Drew and Mandy, the creak of the leather gloves covering his fingers loud in the quiet room.

"Something's happened to your mom," he bent down so that he was more on their level. "But don't worry, I'm gonna bring her back."

Drew's eyes were always the more serious of the two. "I'm counting on you." He sounded so much like an adult that Liam did a double take to make sure he hadn't grown a foot and sprouted a beard. "We've never counted on anybody before," he told Liam, putting his arm around Mandy.

"He's right. Nobody's ever been there for us besides Mom, so we're counting on you to bring her home." Mandy was not usually the serious of the two, but her eyes were as somber as he had ever seen them.

The words those children spoke to him tore at his heart. He knew that he couldn't let them down. He couldn't let Denise down. Now that he'd finally found something worth living for, he couldn't let it slip through his fingers. Liam would not be a quitter the way his mother had quit on him. He would find Richard Joyce and tear him apart limb by limb. Vengeance would be his, and they would never worry about him again.

War had just been declared.

Chapter Twenty-Nine

"You know Liam will come for me."

Denise said it in a sing-song voice because she had no doubt that he would be there soon, guns blazing, pissed the hell off, and ready to take her home. She did it to deliberately taunt the man who had taken her. It pissed her off that he had come into *her* backyard and taken her unwillingly.

Richard glared at the woman, his hard eyes telling her to shut up. Since she had awakened from the chloroform an hour ago, she had not stopped talking. He had listened in the beginning because he hoped that she would say something he could use. Instead, what she had spoken about were things that he already knew. It was now getting on his nerves, and he was starting to get sick of it.

To throw her off, he smirked at her, giving her a wink. "I'm countin' on it darlin'."

The skeevy way he smiled made her want to puke. Was this the man who'd raped Meredith? Was he the one who caused all the issues that were going on with the club right now? What else could she find out? Maybe she could help the club in the way a member's girlfriend normally did.

"Are you gonna rape me the way you raped Meredith?" Her eyes were clear, and she showed no fear as she asked him the thing she wanted to know most.

That question took him aback. "Let's get one thing straight. I didn't rape, nor did I have the reporter raped. I'm surprised that you came right out and asked me that though. Maybe you do have the backbone that I originally didn't think you had. That's pretty ballsy Ms. Cunningham."

Her gut told her that he might be telling the truth, but for some reason she just couldn't let this go. She wanted to do something to help her friend, and at this moment in time this was all she had. "But you know who did? You probably ordered it. Have you been watching us? I mean how else would you know who I am?" The questions poured from her mouth, all things she wanted to know, and all things she felt that he could answer.

"Jesus Christ, how does Liam put up with all your fucking questions? Does he fuck you all day and night just so he doesn't have to listen to you? Shut the fuck up."

The glint of anger in his eyes made her obey him. This man was capable of things she had probably never imagined. She could see that in the way he tightened his fists at his sides. Maybe it would serve her best to do what he said and just wait for the rescue she knew would be coming.

"What does he hope to do taking her?" William asked the group of officers.

"My bet is that he needs money. If he ordered the hit on her and the hit on Meredith, he owes somebody for that. Richard is not one to get his hands dirty," Tyler said quietly.

"So what's he gonna do? Ransom her?" Liam asked.

"Possible," Tyler was thoughtful in his quiet way, probably going over every scenario that they would be faced with.

"I feel like an asshole just sitting around here, not doing anything. We need to be going to where that GPS says she is and get her out. There's no telling what he's done to her," Liam growled. He wanted vengeance, and he wanted it now. He was sick of sitting around, waiting on something to happen. He would be damned if what happened to Meredith happened to Denise when he could prevent it.

"We need a plan." William argued. It was obvious in the way his members were looking at him that he was losing them. Liam was becoming much more of a vocal leader, and they were beginning to follow him without question. William knew that, son or not, he had to get this shit under control.

"Fuck a plan. It's obvious he's getting desperate, which means he'll get sloppy."

William held his hand up. "*We* don't want to be sloppy. *We* want to do this right."

Liam fumed. "None of this has been done right. None of this has been handled. We have one woman missing. We have another lying in a bed beaten, raped, and scared of her shadow. Fuck a bunch of this shit. I'm going. Who's with me?"

He stood up and watched for the other members. Many of them stood up, obviously wanting to be with him.

All battling the bloodlust inside them, wanting to do something to make a difference.

Fighting to keep hold of his club, William banged on the table. "I have not dismissed this meeting yet."

"It's not yours to dismiss. It's *my* old lady he's got, not yours. This is my problem, and I'll fuckin' take care of it." Liam had never openly defied his president at the table, but he felt strongly about this. No one cared more about Denise than he did, and if anyone was going to get her back it would be him. He would crawl through a desert with no water, walk barefoot over a road of glass, but nothing was going to stop him from getting her back to her family where she belonged.

William hissed as he saw everyone behind his son walk out of the meeting. "Shit."

Meredith lay in Tyler's bed trying to convince herself to get up. She'd lain in bed for hours, and it hadn't made her feel any different. She thought that maybe it would make her feel better if she got up and walked around a little bit. Maybe it would lift some of the heavy blanket that felt like it was pressing against her chest. As she contemplated the type of energy it would take in order to do that, the door opened and Tyler walked in.

"I didn't scare you did I?" he asked, walking over to the closet.

She shook her head, shy around him. Why, she wasn't sure, but she couldn't bring herself to look at him. Interested, she watched as he began pulling weapons out of a trunk in the closet and put on a bullet proof vest.

"Where are you going?" she asked quietly. She had never seen someone other than a soldier casually strap on that much armor before. It scared her, and it made her wonder just what in the hell was going on. What had happened in the time she had been out?

He leveled her with a gaze, his brown eyes serious as she had ever seen them. "Some asshole has Denise. We're going to get her back. Hopefully we'll get to her before he can do to her what was done to you."

Shame rolled through her body, and she ducked her head. Nobody should have to live through that and she wanted to tell him that, but she couldn't bring herself to talk to him. The only thing she could bring herself to do was say a little prayer for her friend and hope that whoever this was would have mercy on her.

"We'll be back later," he told her.

Taking out a gun, he checked the chamber and safety. "If someone who is not a part of this club tries to come through that door, you shoot first, ask questions later. Do you understand me? All you gotta do is click the safety off. There's one in the chamber." He flipped it over in her hand to show her how to take the safety off and then laid it on the bed next to her.

She nodded as she picked it up, weighing the heaviness of the gun in her hand. She watched as he left and then had a seat Indian style on the bed. This was the one thing she *could* do. This time she could protect herself if worst came to worst. For the first time in her life, she knew that she wouldn't hesitate to put another human being down if it came to that. It gave her a power that she needed, and she knew that she would do whatever she had to.

"I figured your old man would be here by now," Richard taunted Denise as she sat tied up in a chair. He sat on a chair directly across from her. He was straddling the back, feigning indifference as he loosely held a gun in his hands, but she could tell by the bunching of his shoulder muscles that he was beginning to feel nervous.

In truth she had too, but she wasn't worried. "I'm sure he's trying to think of the most interesting way to kill you," she smiled her most bitchy smile at him.

"He'll have to come here first, won't he? Maybe he's decided that you aren't worth it. How does that make you feel?" Richard couldn't help but needle her. Liam Walker had never been able to commit to just one woman, and Richard couldn't see him doing it now either. Not with *this* woman.

"I'm fine, at least I didn't get kicked out of my club," she taunted him in return.

That stung. She really was a bitch. "Shut your damn mouth," he growled as he backhanded her across the face with the butt of his gun.

"You're really gonna wish you hadn't done that," she told him, spitting out blood that was already pouring into her mouth from where she had bitten her lip.

He leaned the chair forward so that they were nose to nose. "You're gonna wish you'd never gotten involved with the Heaven Hill MC." He raised his hand to hit her again when the door exploded and members of the club rushed through, guns blazing.

Liam, throwing caution to the wind, ran over to where Richard hovered above her and grabbed him by the collar of the shirt, rocking the chair so far back that Richard's head almost hit the concrete floor. "You are a miserable piece of shit, you son of a bitch."

"Now, Liam, I have a business proposition for you. I just need some cash to help get it off the ground." Richard held his hands up in surrender and had the nerve to laugh, letting the gun fall to the ground.

Grinning at the older man, Liam made sure his fist connected with Richard's face. It felt good to cause him pain, it felt gratifying as his knuckles cracked over the bones in Richard's body. "This is where you can take your damn business proposition."

For long minutes, the two of them beat the absolute shit out of each other while Tyler freed Denise. She shrieked as Richard landed a blow to Liam's ribs.

"Let them go. He's got it coming to him after this," he said calmly, holding her back.

She watched as Liam got the upper hand and then picked up the older man, slamming him face first into a concrete wall. Liam was strong, but she had no idea he was *that* strong. It was amazing what adrenaline did for someone.

"Did you get rid of it, or when I rip this shirt off of you are you going to still have it?" Liam spat, breathing heavily, blood spilling from his mouth.

It struck Denise that they had matching battle wounds. Surely that proved to everyone just how serious she was about this man.

Richard groaned, rolling his head around on his shoulders. Liam ripped the shirt from his body and showed the rest of the club what Richard hadn't gotten rid of. He still wore the tattoos of the Heaven Hill MC. The sleeves covered his arms.

Liam slapped his back, his gloved hands making the sound muted. "Don't worry, Dickey boy, we'll take care of you."

Tyler handed Denise over to a Prospect. "Get her out of here."

"What are they going to do?" she asked the Prospect, Layne she thought was his name.

"Get back their respect and then take care of the problem," he told her softly. He had never been present at anything like that, but he knew the code of the club and he knew just how bad of a deal it was that Richard still wore the ink.

"They're going to kill him?"

"Only after he wishes he was already dead," Layne confirmed, leading her out of the building and to a waiting van so that she wouldn't see anything.

He immediately took her back to the clubhouse, where Drew and Mandy stood, their arms wrapped around one another. Tears clogged Denise's throat as she caught sight of the worry on their faces. She hadn't meant to cause that worry – had never meant for any of this to happen.

"Mom," Mandy screamed as she ran to the van, helping Denise open the door. All Denise could do was open her arms and let the girl fall into them. In his own stoic way, Drew stood to the side, waiting for the emotions of the girls to die down. Much like he had done his whole life, he waited until there was an opening and then he put his arms around the both of them, holding them tightly.

As she looked at her children, she was excited to know that she would be around to see them grow up. However, at the same time, Denise felt sorrow, but not for the man who had done so many bad things to other people. She felt sorrow because she assumed the identity of Meredith's rapist died with this man. It hurt her heart that they would never get revenge for her, but she couldn't say that this man didn't deserve to die. With him, maybe old hurts and secrets would go too. Maybe now they could all start anew.

Chapter Thirty

The sun was just beginning to break the horizon as Liam walked out of the warehouse that Denise had been held in. In his nostrils, he could still smell the burning flesh that had been Richard Joyce. When a member decided not to get rid of his ink after leaving the club, the club did it for him. This particular time, Liam had taken great pleasure in cutting the ink up into sections and then burning it off. He would be lying if he didn't admit that it had felt good and that's what worried him.

For the first time in his life, Liam felt bad about what he had done in the name of his club. He felt as if he wasn't worthy enough to go home and sleep with the woman who warmed up the other side of his bed. He worried that she would look at him differently. Hell, he knew after this he would look at himself different. Never before had he felt such euphoria as he had done something so heinous. It scared him in a way – he didn't want to be *that* man.

"You okay?" Tyler asked as he tipped a bottle of water over their hands, trying to clean as much blood off them as they could before the ride back to the clubhouse.

"Yeah, but I'm feeling some remorse – not for killing him – but how is Denise going to look at me now? And I felt *good* doing that. What does that say about me?" Liam ran his hands down his jeans, rubbing some of the water off.

Tyler, intelligent as always, leveled him with a stare. "She knew who you were when she got into this relationship with you."

Liam knew that Tyler spoke the truth, but he also knew that it was easy to overlook truths as long as they weren't staring you in the face. She had been witness to this first hand tonight.

"I know, but I hated doing that in front of her. I feel like she knows me as one way when I'm with her, but when I'm with you guys I turn into a different person. Things that shouldn't feel right do, and that's scary for someone who trusts me with her children. I can't even say I'm comfortable with the animal that came out of me tonight," Liam admitted. With Tyler he knew that he could be completely honest without repercussion.

"None of us felt good about it. At one time he was a friend, a brother, but we have to do what we have to do sometimes. In those hours that we did that, had he admitted to being behind Meredith's rape, I would have snapped and broken his neck. Without thought. Without a doubt. Without remorse. We are who we are brother, there's a little bit of warrior in all of us. That makes us who we are." Tyler always knew what to say, almost like he knew what Liam was going to say before he said it.

"This is the first time I've ever had to worry about what a woman would say. It's really the first time I've worried what anyone would say. I'm trying to keep a part of myself while I try to be what this club needs, but I worry that I'm in a losing battle. I don't want her to look at me with fear in her eyes. That's the last thing I want."

Tyler put his hand on his friend's back. "Something tells me that Denise understood this. She saw what Meredith looked like. I think she's okay with it, and if she's not then the two of you work on it. A relationship is about checks and balances. It's about coming to terms with what makes it work for both parties, not just one. I think she'll surprise you."

"Guess we'll find out won't we?"

Denise lay in Liam's dorm room, waiting for him to come back. She wondered what they would say to each other, if things would be different. The brutality he had used to attack Richard's body hadn't surprised her, but it had made her think of him as a different kind of man. Now she thought of him the way she did Tyler. It wasn't bad – just different.

The door opened quietly, and she knew by the footfalls that it was Liam. Quickly, she threw her legs over the side of the bed and raced to him. He caught her in his arms and held her tightly to his body, inhaling deeply and moving his hands to her hair, caressing her head and neck softly. The softness of the hands holding her reminded her just how different he was when they were alone and when it was about them.

"I'm so glad you're okay," she whispered, holding him tightly against her, snaking her arms around his neck.

"I'm okay? Hell, you took fifteen years off my life when I came back and realized you weren't here," his voice hoarse with emotion. That was how she knew he was the man she thought he was. Someone callous couldn't care about her so much it made his voice crack. That wasn't faked emotion. That was as real as it got.

With strong hands he picked her up, carrying her over to the bed and sitting her down. Kneeling in front of her, he ran his hands along her body, checking to make sure everything was there and accounted for. Tenderly, he ran the back of his hand along the bruise that had already formed on her cheek. Then he carefully touched the spot where her lip had split from the impact with the gun.

"I'm good as long as you're good," she whispered to him.

"I'm so far from good right now, but it's because of what was done to you. This could have ended up so much differently. You could be where Meredith is right now." His eyes were red with emotion, and he tried valiantly not to let that emotion spill over.

"I'm not, thanks to you. You got to me in time. I knew you would. I never doubted that. I had complete faith in you and your ability to *not* let me end up like Meredith."

"Thank God for that," he breathed, bringing his hand up to the back of her head and holding her tightly against him.

Quietly, she asked the question he had been dreading. "Did you kill him?"

"I had to. He disrespected you, and he disrespected the club. There's certain protocol that has to be followed. He's lucky I didn't castrate him before all was said and done. I've never felt that kind of anger or rage before," he told her, moving back so that she could see his eyes. "I've always been able to stop myself before I got too far, but seeing him there with you, the blood on your face and knowing that he had done that to you. I couldn't stop myself."

She put her hands up. "You don't have to explain yourself to me. I wanted to kill him with my bare hands too. I don't think he's the one that raped Meredith, but I still think he had something to do with it. I really wanted to at least get that out of him, but he wouldn't answer me when I asked more questions. I'll always regret that."

"Jesus Christ. You asked him about it? Were you trying to get yourself killed?" His heart beat rapidly as he realized for a second time just how close he had been to losing her. Richard wasn't a patient man, and he had obviously showed great restraint when it came to her questions.

She tilted her chin up in defiance. "I was just trying to help a friend. I know she would have done the same for me. We need to know who did this. She shouldn't have to live in fear. If I can do anything for her, I will. Don't take away the backbone I seem to have found."

"I won't," he bit his lip, bringing his hands up to her face. "I love it about you."

Her heart stopped and she grinned. "I love you too, Liam."

"This may not ever be conventional," he warned. In fact he never expected it to be, but he still had to warn her.

"I know, and I'm not expecting it to be. I've known that since the beginning."

He framed her face with his large hands, bringing their lips together in a kiss meant to ignite every part of her body. He bent to pick her up off the bed, and she wrapped her legs around his body, allowing his hands to support her weight. She brought her hands to his cut and began to remove it when a knock sounded.

"Fuck," he swore. "What?"

Tyler's deep voice came through the door. "We need our VP to go over the information we just found out about Richard."

"Really?" he mumbled. "I'll be there in a few minutes."

She giggled as he buried his face in her neck and sighed, using his tongue to lick a path around to her lips. The hot breath tickled where her hair moved.

"You go do what you gotta do. I'll still be here," she promised.

"Hopefully this won't take very long. Besides, before we even get to taking our clothes off we need showers. I've got blood all over me and so do you."

She looked down, realizing he was speaking the truth. For the first time she felt like his equal, not someone that he had to take care of. She had done a damn good job of taking care of herself until he could come rescue her. The knowledge that she could stand on her own two feet and be strong after everything that had happened to her was the best gift anyone would have given her, and she had Liam to thank for that.

"Show me what ya got," William commanded Steele and Jagger Stone as they sat around their large table.

Steele pulled out a binder full of paper and spread the sheets out in front of him. "It looks like the business that Richard wanted to discuss with us was running guns. He apparently has a contact from Louisville, and they're running guns down south to the Mexican Cartel."

Liam whistled between his teeth. "That's some big time shit. Is that really something we wanna get involved in? We get caught and that's Federal time. I'm all for protection runs, but I don't want our fingerprints on this."

"Maybe it's time to diversify," Tyler shrugged from where he sat next to Liam.

"Drugs aren't what they used to be," William put his thoughts out there. "Any redneck with an empty double-wide and a package of cold medicine can make meth. We don't have the monopoly on drugs the way we used to anyway. Hard times are coming, and we need to make sure we can stay solvent."

"So what do we do?" Liam asked. "Just tell these people that we killed Richard, and now we want in on it?"

"Why not?" Jagger asked. He was young and reminded Liam of Meredith because when he wanted something, he went after it without thinking of consequences.

"He's got a point," Steele shrugged. "I mean obviously they need to move this product. There could be some big money in it. Big enough that we could completely move out of drugs."

"So we can *really* become one percenter's then?"

"Times are what they are," William argued. "Let's put it up for a vote. All in favor of seeing what we can do with these guns?"

Everyone raised their hands quickly except for Liam. After glancing around at the table, he knew he had to back his brothers on this. Regardless of what he thought, they still had to earn, and they had to do that any way that they could.

William banged his gavel. "That passed, so we'll look into it and let you know what's going on. Steele and Jagger, you two get this off the ground. If you need help, let me or Liam know."

This was a bad idea. Liam knew it, but there was nothing he could do about it. It would have to play out however it would play out. The club was changing, and he guessed he would just have to change with it. The mark of a good leader was rolling with punches, and he was beginning to learn to do just that.

Chapter Thirty-One

After the meeting adjourned, Liam was trying to make his way back to his dorm room, only to be stopped by the one person he didn't want to see. Lauren. He averted his eyes, hoping it would show her just how much he *didn't* want to talk to her.

"Liam, I would really love the chance to be able to sit down and talk to you," she told him softly, reaching out to touch his elbow lightly.

He pulled his elbow back, almost like her touch burned him. "Right now is *not* the time," he bit out as coldly as he could.

"There's never a good time for you," she argued. "All I want is a chance to explain my side of things. There are always two sides to every story, Liam. I think you owe me that much."

He finally looked at her, really looked at her, and he felt remorse for the way he was treating the woman had given birth to him. After dealing with Richard, he knew that he could change things in his life. He didn't have to be a bastard to everyone. He didn't *want* to be a bastard to everyone. Maybe this was his chance to alter the way their relationship had been for so long. Being with Denise had changed everything. He would never allow Drew to talk to his mother the way he talked to Lauren. Purposely, he softened his voice.

"Look, right now seriously isn't a good time." Did he tell his mom he was in a hurry to get back to his dorm and get laid? He needed to be with Denise more than he could breathe at this moment, he needed to prove to himself that everything was okay and they were going to make it. "But how about tomorrow or even later on tonight. I promise you, I will make time. We *will* talk."

"That's all I'm asking for. You can even have that woman you care for so much with you, if you want. If she's the reason for your change of heart, then I want her there. You've changed, and it's for the better," she told him, her blue eyes the mirror image of his.

"We'll see," he relented. "I'll come find you. I promise, Mom."

Tears came to her eyes. He hadn't called her Mom since she'd left. Even as a six-year-old, he'd called her Lauren. "I'll hold you to that."

He took a minute to put his hand in hers and give it a gentle squeeze. Not for false hope, but because he actually did have hope this time. Maybe things would change and they could move on.

It took him a while, but when he finally got back to his dorm, he opened the door only to find Denise nowhere in sight. He didn't think she had left, there was still a presence in the room.

"Denise?" he called out.

"In here," he heard her from the bathroom.

As he got to the bathroom, he heard the shower running. Sick of waiting, he began disrobing. He'd be damned if he would let anyone interrupt them this time. Thinking better of it, he turned around and flipped the lock on the bedroom door before all but running for the bathroom.

He stepped in the shower behind Denise and circled his arms around her body.

"I was beginning to think you forgot about me," she grumbled good-naturedly before turning under the spray so that they could face one another.

"I'd never forget about this," he whispered as he leaned in to nip at her lips with his.

The look on his face was so serious it gave her goose bumps. There was no hint of joking around or taking any of this lightly. Not that there would be any of that this deep in the game, but she still had trouble believing that this was real even after the events from earlier. Their relationship was in the infant stages, and she was learning so much about him. It was hard to recognize the facets of the man in front of her. He was happy-go-lucky at times, chill and laid back at others, but sometimes he was so serious that it scared her. Needing to feel close to him, she shoved her fingers through his hair and pulled his mouth down to hers. His hands came around her backside and cupped her ass, using his leverage to pick her up. On instinct, she wrapped her legs around his waist, moaning as she came into contact with the evidence of his arousal.

"You love going all caveman on me, don't you?"

His blue eyes glowed, and the corner of his mouth tilted in amusement. "You love it when I go all caveman, don't act like you don't."

She shivered as he pressed her against the cold tile of the shower, bringing their bodies closer together. "That I do," she moaned as he leaned her back slightly. Just before her breasts, he stopped and lifted his head, his eyes pinning her with a hard gaze. The beard on his face gave him a dangerous edge and his forehead creased as he bent his head and used his teeth to tease her nipple. She opened her mouth at the sharp prick of pain before he used the flat of his tongue to soothe the ache.

The sound of water beating down on them roared in her ears as she held on tightly to his shoulders, giving him free reign as he held her upper back in his strong hands. It allowed her to lean even further backward, giving her a feeling of being weightless. Out of the blue, the water went cold, causing her to shriek, bringing her out of the haze of pleasure he'd weaved around them.

"You're gonna love this," he promised.

Already their body heat was turning the water warmer, and she had to admit the bite of the cold was arousing. It caused her already hard nipples to stiffen further as the coolness trailed down her body. She couldn't help but writhe against him, trying to coax him inside the warmth of her core.

"What about shrinkage?" she challenged, her eyes teasing.

"I don't think we'll have a problem with that," he growled, plunging into her body. He pulled her as close as they could be, trailing open mouth kisses down the column of her throat, making noises as she squeezed around him.

She groaned as the cold water invaded the heat of her body. It was exciting, the difference in temperatures. Much more arousing than she had ever imagined. Her fingers flexed on his biceps as she pushed them apart. Immediately his mouth covered the tip of her nipple and his cheeks hollowed when he sucked sharply. Again the feeling of his warm mouth around the icy coldness of her skin caused her breath to hitch. Never before had she done anything like this, and the unknown was almost as arousing as the feelings he made course through her body.

Tightening her legs around his waist, she spurred him on, wanting to feel the fullness that only he could give her.

"You like that?" he asked as he shoved roughly inside of her.

She nodded, bringing her lip up between her teeth.

"I can't hear you baby, you gotta tell me." He pulled out, leaving just the tip of his cock inside her, teasing as he waited for her to tell him what he wanted to hear.

"I like it," she whispered.

"You like what?"

Damn him. He wasn't making this easy for her. It wasn't like her to tell him exactly what she wanted, exactly what she liked. Hell, she was still learning what she liked if she were honest with herself.

"I like everything that you do to me. I like feeling your cock deep inside me," she whispered, heat coming to her face.

"Yeah?" he asked, griping her hips tighter in his hands.

"Oh yeah," she answered back.

The flat of his hand took her by surprise as he smacked it against the flesh of her ass, causing her to let out a garbled moan. He loved that sound she made it when she got some sort of unexpected pleasure. It made him harder, just thinking about the fact that he was the man to give her that pleasure, to wrench that noise from her throat.

"C'mon baby," he urged her on. Bracing her body tighter against the wet wall of the shower, he moved one of his hands down to her core and rubbed his finger along the hard nub of her clit. "Fall apart for me," he coaxed her, not sure how much longer he would be able to keep up the punishing pace he had set.

Denise bucked her hips against his finger and the hardness of his cock slicing her in half. He could feel her tightening, and he fought valiantly to hold off his own explosion. The effort caused him to tighten his abs, his ass, and his arms. She opened her eyes, seeing his teeth clenched.

It was that display of maleness that sent her over the edge. The thought of him trying to hold himself together so tightly for *her* pleasure. It set off every feminine trigger in her body.

"Oh God," she cried, tears springing to her eyes at the emotions that erupted within her.

Liam buried his head in her neck and bit down sharply, sucking as he spilled himself inside her. Lethargy immediately swamped his body, and he fought to lift his head. The steam from the shower swirled around them causing him to close and open his eyes swiftly, trying to focus.

"You wore me out," he accused, not moving his head from her shoulder.

"No, I'm pretty sure you wore me out," she laughed, gingerly removing her legs from around his waist.

He cautiously sat her down, waiting to see if her legs would support her after being in that position for so long.

When they buckled, his large hands grasped her hips and held her still for a few moments. As he kept her body close to his, he reached over and turned the warmth of the shower back on as they concentrated on regulating their breathing. She stomped her feet a few times against the floor, hoping to get feeling back into her legs.

"You are a force to be reckoned with," she giggled.

His smile was purely masculine. She did things to him that no other woman ever had. Made him feel like such a man, like he could lift a car with his bare hands or break a steel plated door. The feeling wasn't one he ever wanted to go away. His eyes traveled over her body, admiring the way the water slid over every nook and cranny, getting himself all worked up again. As he lifted his gaze to her neck, he cursed softly.

"What?" she asked, bringing her hand up to the spot where her neck and shoulder met. The place where his eyes were now looking so intently.

"How do you feel about being the mother of thirteen-year-old twins and having a hickey?"

Her eyes bugged, and her mouth dropped open. "You gave me a hickey? I've never in my life had a hickey," he could hear the panic in her voice.

"Well, you do now," he told her, trying to hide the smile that spread across his face.

"I'm not sure how I feel about this. A hickey after my teenage years. I need to see how trashy it looks."

As he got them out of the shower, he couldn't help the swell of pride he felt. "That's my mark of ownership."

"I think everybody got that *before* you gave me the hickey," she joked.

He walked them over to the sink and stood behind her as they looked in the mirror. He used his hand to tilt her head to the side, admiring his handy work. "That's fuckin' hot."

"Men," she blushed. "I will never understand."

Chapter Thirty-Two

Lauren watched her son as he came out of his dorm room the next morning, his hand firmly clasping Denise's. The tension and wariness that had been tightly wound into his body the night before was no longer there. The large hickey that was present on the woman's neck was proof of just how he had relaxed. Truth be told she couldn't remember the last time he had walked around without tension in his shoulders and his eyes shifting this way and that. It saddened her that she'd never seen her son like this before.

"What do you say we grab some breakfast and go sit outside?" he asked as he ambled up to her. He seemed at peace with himself, much more comfortable in his body than she could ever remember him being.

She looked into his eyes, trying to gauge whether he really wanted to give her a second chance at being his mother. Her heart couldn't take it if he wasn't truly interested in this. What she saw there made her hopeful. It looked as if he wanted this as much as she did. "That's fine with me. Is your lady coming with us?"

The look he bestowed on Denise was one of pure adoration and love. To be honest, it made Lauren jealous.

Even early on in her marriage to William, he had *never* looked at her like that. Liam pulled her hand to his lips and kissed the palm. "If she wants, and if you don't care."

"I don't. I would love it if you would come with us." Lauren was eager for anything that would allow her a few precious moments with the son she didn't know. Anything that would move their relationship forward.

Denise smiled prettily, "Then I would love to."

The trio walked into the kitchen and caught a glimpse of Tyler sitting at the table, a coffee cup in front of him. If she wasn't mistaken, that coffee cup looked like an amazingly real replica of a skull. His face was serious like it always was, and Denise could see lines of fatigue around his eyes and mouth.

"How's Meredith?" she asked, gasping as he lifted the cup up to his mouth and took a sip. It was, in fact, what she assumed it was. A small skull, but a skull nonetheless.

He shuddered as the caffeine coursed through his body. He hoped like hell this would wake him up because he had spent most of the previous night sitting in watch over Meredith. "Rough night and what's wrong with you?"

"Is that a skull?" she asked, her brows knitting together. "It looks disturbingly real. Is it?"

He smiled. She'd never seen the man smile before and it completely changed his face. It made her want to do anything he asked. It was very disconcerting, and she almost chuckled as Liam came up behind her and put an arm around her shoulder. For the first time it was obvious that Tyler was the 'make your panties drop' man of the group. Funny, she hadn't pegged him as that man before.

"People assume that because I'm Native American it is, but no one really knows for sure," his eyes twinkled with mischief.

"Liam is it real?" She asked, tilting her head to the side with the question.

"Don't know, darlin'. He won't even tell me. He plays things close to the vest sometimes. He just smiles at people and tells them that it may or may not be cursed."

"You mean he's your best friend and he doesn't tell you everything?" She asked, leaning back to look him in the eye.

"We're not a bunch of girls, baby. We're men, we don't *have* to tell each other everything. There's nothing wrong with keeping some things a mystery."

She frowned. That wasn't at all the answer she was looking for. Denise really wanted to know if it was cursed or not.

Liam grabbed her hand and lead her out of the kitchen, having gotten breakfast while she contemplated the presumed cursed skull coffee cup. Curious still, she looked back at the big man and shivered when he winked at her. It was pretty obvious he would never tell.

Outside on the back porch, the three of them sat in relative silence eating breakfast. Denise's stomach churned, not sure how this would work out for Liam. He was hurt because of things that had happened in the past, and that she understood. But as a mother herself, she also understood that sometimes things just were. You couldn't gauge how your kids would react to everything, and sometimes split decisions had to be made. She hoped with everything in her that the both of them – Liam and Lauren – could come through this with a little better understanding of each other.

"Before you say anything," Lauren began. "Can I explain to you where I came from as your mother?"

Denise felt the tension roll off Liam's body, so she reached over and grabbed his hand. The gentle squeeze she gave told him that he had to be patient. He had to hear her side before he went off half-cocked. Because he would expect Drew to give his own mother that much respect, he cleared his throat and shifted. "Go ahead,"

"When your Dad and I got married, I didn't sign on to be an old lady. I signed on to be his wife. Sure he'd always liked motorcycles and the culture, but I never once thought he would want to embrace it or live it. I was used to us going to the get-togethers and then coming home and being a family. I didn't expect what all this entailed. For a while I was okay with it. The club was our main source of income in the middle to late '70s. It put food on the table, but there wasn't all this illegal shit going on. When we had Sharon, I breathed a sigh of relief. A daughter wasn't going to be expected to take over an MC. She might be expected to be with a member, but the legacy is not going to be hers."

As a mother herself, Denise got where this was going. It was going to hurt Liam, she was sure, but she could understand where his mother was coming from. Knowing he would need compassion, she rubbed his hand softly, hoping to calm him down. Denise felt sorrow for the two of them. She could almost bet how this was going to play out.

Lauren fought back tears as her chin quivered. It was going to hurt her deeply to say the next words, but she knew that she had to make Liam understand. Only with the truth could there be understanding. She had learned that lesson the hard way over the years.

"When I had you, my world ended. The day you came home from the hospital, your Dad started talking about grooming you. They were starting to get into the illegal side of things, and the only thing I could think of was that you'd never have a life. I couldn't bring myself to be as close to you as I was to Sharon. I knew that one day you'd be taken from me. I knew that one day I would have to hand you over to this club, and I couldn't bear it. I couldn't bear the thought of you not being my little boy anymore. I'm sure you don't remember, but I tried to do other things with you that didn't involve the club. One day when I took you to the Science Museum in Nashville, you came home and told William you wanted to be an astronaut. That was the first time he beat me." Lauren struggled through this part, not particularly wanting to tell Liam what stock he came from. But again, she had learned the truth would set her free.

Denise could see Liam's teeth clench and his jaw tighten. This was hard for him. Not that he had any illusions about William, but he really did not like violence towards women if it could be helped. She reached over and put her hand on his thigh, offering her support. It appeared to be equally hard for Lauren as she fought valiantly against the tears that streaked her face.

"He told me that your legacy was this club. You were to have no other dreams, and if I couldn't get on board with that, then I could leave. I was to leave you and Sharon and never look back. I'm sure you don't remember. You were so young. I really hope you don't remember in hindsight. We left that night. I grabbed all our stuff and even took just you, not Sharon. Just you, Liam. I knew that if I left you here, he would destroy all the good things that made you the sweet little boy you were. We ran for two days until William and the club caught up to us. Let's just say it wasn't pretty. Not wanting any more harm to come to you, I decided as a mother that loved you the best thing I could do was leave."

Leaning over, Denise placed her hand on his shoulder and whispered in his ear. "She does love you. She did everything for you. Please tell me you can understand that."

When she pulled away, this big man had tears in his eyes and his bottom lip quivered. He sniffed heavily. "I don't remember any of that," he whispered, coughing loudly to cover up his display of emotion.

"I know, and I don't blame you at all, Liam. You were a child. I made a decision. It was never about right or wrong, because the decision I made wasn't truthfully right. Any mother worth anything would not have left her child. I regret it every day, especially when I see the man you've become. I know I had no hand in that."

"He's a good man," Denise defended. No matter what they saw him do as the VP of the club, he was such a different person when they were alone. So tender, and emotional, and willing to be the type of man she had always wanted as the father to her children.

"He is," Lauren agreed. "But this club is going to eat him up and spit him out before long. I don't know that he has the heart to do the things they will eventually ask him to do."

It scared Liam because he'd always thought that of himself too. He'd hoped he'd hidden it well within the club. He'd never backed down from anything, but it always weighed heavily on his mind.

"I'll always do what I have to do."

Lauren scooted forward and tentively grabbed her son's hand. "But at what cost, Liam?"

"Whatever the cost is, I have to pay it. When you left me here, this became my legacy. I've done too much to walk away now," he explained as gently as he could. "Like you said, decisions were made. None of them were good. Now I have to live with it, and I'm okay with that."

"I'm not," Lauren whispered.

It took everything in Liam's body to say the words that came out of his mouth next. "Mom, I forgive you, and I understand now. Maybe we can work on having a relationship."

"I would like that very much," her smile shook.

Denise fought back her own show of emotion as the two of them embraced for the first time in nearly twenty-five years. She was happy she'd been able to be a part of this. It had meant the world to her.

"Did you work everything out with your mother?"

Liam saw red as he saw his dad for the first time since the conversation he'd had with said mother. Walking up to him, he balled his fist and hit him with everything he had carried around, causing the older man's head to snap back.

"The fuck?" he yelled, spitting out blood.

"How could you do that? How could you make a mother choose?"

William turned on his wife quickly. "What kind of mother even chooses?"

"You're not doing this to me now. I'm not a little kid that you can play like a guitar anymore. Our relationship – if you can even call it that – will never be the same, Dad." He spit the last word out with thinly veiled disgust.

"I did the best I could," William argued.

"No, you did what was best for the club," Liam roared.

Liam knew in that moment that things would have to change. Club and family were interchangeable but at some point a man had to put his family first. It was time to make some changes with the younger generation. He had to make them see what they would be giving up if they didn't think about life outside of the club.

"I chose to keep you when she threw you away."

"That you did Dad, but you didn't give a shit about your son and don't think I'll ever forget that."

Epilogue

A few days later, Liam and Denise sat on the sun porch of what she'd finally started to call their house. It was late, almost midnight, and the kids had finally gone to bed. This had become their favorite time of day. Late at night after everything had settled down, they'd taken to coming out on the porch and discussing their day. Sometimes it was just a discussion, sometimes it led to more. Whatever it ended up being, Denise loved it no matter what.

"Anything interesting happen today?" he asked, pulling her close to his chest, relishing the way her head fit under his chin.

"Your Mom called. She said they have a job opening at the courthouse in the same department she's in."

It hadn't been a bad idea when Lauren pitched it to her, but Denise had been unsure of how Liam would take it. She still wasn't very sure what her role in his life was besides companion.

"The courthouse, huh? With my Mom? What do you think about that?"

"I dunno," she shrugged. "My first thought was maybe I could help the club. Ya know? There's a lot of things I can find out in that office," she laughed.

"You *so* deserve what I'm about to give you," he laughed along with her. That was the hallmark of a good woman in his circle. Always thinking about what she could do to help the club.

"A good hard fucking?" she asked cheekily.

"And such a dirty mouth on you too? What happened to the meek woman you were when I first met you?"

"You brought out her wild side," she whispered, running her tongue along his jawline.

"I'm glad, but sit tight right here for just a second."

He got up from where they sat and made his way into the house. She twirled her thumbs, wondering exactly what he was doing. Listening carefully, she heard him open the closet door in the hallway where the jackets were kept. It was a warm night, she wasn't sure why he would need a jacket.

"Close your eyes," he called as he made his way back out onto the porch. His voice was pitched high, obviously excited to show her what he had brought her.

She did as he asked and sat, waiting for whatever it was he was going to give her. For some reason her heart beat wildly against her chest. Nobody had ever given her anything before. He sat something gently beside her, and then the couch dipped as he sat on the other side.

"Open 'em up!"

It took a moment for her eyes to re-adjust to the darkness. When she saw a pink box, wrapped in a bow, her hand flew to her mouth. "What'd you do?" she asked, suspicion in her eyes.

"Guess you'll have to open it to find out won't you?"

Not wanting to admit that she'd never had a gift from another man before, she took her time. She savored opening the bow and then the paper. She could see the excitement in his eyes, and it made her want to just tear into it. He held his hands in his lap, almost like he was trying to keep himself from tearing it open for her. As she took the lid off the box, the musky smell of leather hit her nostrils, and she inhaled deeply.

"Seriously?" she asked as she moved back the tissue paper.

"Just wait until you see it," his grin was contagious and she knew she wore one that matched.

She gasped as she finally pulled all the paper back, revealing a bunch of black leather. She wasn't sure if it was a jacket or chaps or what, but her hands shook as ran her fingers over the smooth material.

"Pick it up and get a good look at it," he instructed her.

What she thought was a leather jacket was actually a cut. It had her name stitched into it and below it sat a property patch. She sat it down on her thigh and ran her hand over the patch, trying to hide how much it shook.

Property of William Walker Jr. "Liam"

"Wow," she whispered as she turned it around. The cut had its own colors and patches. It almost made her look like a full-fledged member.

"I also got you some leather chaps to wear. I'm hoping maybe you'll wear nothing but those one night," he teased, popping his eyebrows up and down.

That little shot of humor was needed. A property patch – from what she had seen – was a big deal, but she still needed him to explain to her exactly what he wanted.

"We'll see," she grinned at him. "So what does this mean?" she asked, holding the cut up.

"That you're mine, and no one's ever going to take you away from me. It means when the time is right I'll get you a ring, and we'll make it official in front of God and everybody. How does that sound?"

"Sounds amazing," she breathed deeply, finally content with the direction her life was taking.

Wordlessly he opened his arms to her, and she went into them, settling back against his chest. She could feel the steady beat of his heart, the warmth of his body, and she could feel his hands as they stroked her body. It was the quiet moments like this that she loved the most. The wild man who had turned her on to her own wild side. The man who had accepted her kids as his own and the man who had completely changed her life.

"I'm really lucky that Sharon asked you to work for her," he whispered softly in her ear. Their lives could have gone so much differently had she not answered that call or refused to help out a friend.

She giggled softly. "You don't know how happy I am that I answered that phone call because I almost didn't. I thought it was a bill collector and came pretty damn close to rejecting it, but something told me not to. It was obviously meant to be."

The End

About the Author

Laramie Briscoe has loved romance novels since her grandmother gave her Dorothy Garlock's *Tenderness* as a teenager. It sparked a love of reading and writing that's manifested into this series of novels.

An avid TV and movie enthusiast, a nail polish hoarder, an obsessive book reader, and a lover of all things that sparkle and glitter. She lives in South Central Kentucky with her husband and her cat.

If you enjoyed the story, please post reviews at GoodReads.

I love to hear from fans! Please feel free to contact me at any of the following:

Email:
laramie.briscoe@gmail.com

Facebook:
https://www.facebook.com/AuthorLaramieBriscoe

Facebook:
https://www.facebook.com/HeavenHillRomanceSeries

Pinterest:
http://pinterest.com/laramiebriscoe/

Twitter:
https://twitter.com/LaramieBriscoe

Acknowledgements

There are so many people who helped me on the journey to seeing this project through and I'm going to try and thank all of them. If I forget you, it's because there have been so many, not because I meant to forget you!

My beta readers: Allison, Shellie, Sue, and Amy. Thank you for being honest – even when it may have hurt my feelings – and loving my characters as much as I do!

My dear friend April who has listened to me talk about this for years! She's always there when I need someone to talk to or when I need a traveling partner. Everyone truly needs a friend like her!

My family who is nothing but supportive!

The co-workers of my day job. For a long time none of them had any idea what I was doing, but when I finally told them, they have been nothing but sweet and supportive. They have no idea how much I appreciate it!

Lindsay Hopper and Kari Ayasha: I'm so lucky to have found some amazing people to work with. I'll never forget the chance you took on me and I hope that sometime in the future I am able to repay you for all your kindness.

Fellow author Allison Jewell: We talk about some of the craziest things that no one else but us would understand (usually involving our 'fake' characters). I couldn't have decided to do this with anyone else. We've been through a lot in the last year and a half trying to get this going – personal and professional. Thank you for never letting me give up when I really wanted to and continuing to encourage me, even when I felt like everything else in my life was bigger than this dream.

Everyone else that encouraged me in some way: Anicee, Becky, the KIW, DJFFO, Lesslie, Carol, and Pam - thank you!

Coming Soon

Out of Darkness (Heaven Hill Series #2)

Chapter One

For services rendered.

Meredith awoke sharply, feeling the dollar bill hit her again. It was the same dream every time. She always woke up when he said those words and he threw the dollar bill. Sleep never came with her and stayed with her, even when she took the pills the good doc had prescribed. Carefully, she pushed back the covers of Tyler's bed and slid her legs to the side. Her heart caught the way it always did when she saw Tyler asleep on the floor. Maybe one day she'd be able to invite him into this bed. Quietly, she dressed and grabbed her running shoes. If she couldn't sleep, she may as well get something accomplished.

Making her way to the kitchen of the clubhouse, she smiled and waved at those who had come to know her in the weeks she'd been staying her. It was easy to pretend with these people that nothing really had happened to her. She'd taken a leave of absence from her job and moved all her stuff into storage. Meredith had known without a doubt that she could never go back to the life that she'd had before. Any of it.

"Going for a run?" Liam asked as he spotted her running shoes.

"Yeah, is Denise up yet?"

The look that overtook his face when she mentioned his woman made Meredith sad. She had wanted that at one time and she wasn't sure she'd ever get back to that place in her life.

"Sure is, she was on her way up here. Just text her, I know she'd love to run with you."

It went without saying that Meredith didn't like to run by herself and Denise usually went along whether she wanted to or not. The sign of what Meredith was beginning to understand as being a real friend.

"Will you let Tyler know where I am?" she asked, grabbing a couple bottles of water.

"I will, but you and I both know that he *always* knows where you are."

Not long after her attack, he'd installed a special tracking program on her phone. Before it would have freaked her out, now though, it made her feel safe.

"See ya," she called to the VP as she made her way out the back door.

As she stepped into the sunlight, she looked up. It was coming upon late October in South Central Kentucky and it should have been at least a little bit chilly, but they were in the grips of an Indian summer. For reasons she couldn't understand, Meredith was glad. She wasn't sure she could face a winter being cooped up right now. Being outside in this guarded place was the only way she felt safe. The only time she felt alive besides when she wrote.

Writing had become her solace. She wrote something every day. The doctor had suggested it and she had been amazed at how much she enjoyed it. Although she'd been a reporter, she'd never really been a writer. She loved it even more than the news.

"You ready girlfriend?"

Meredith smiled, the first genuine one she'd had all day as she spotted Denise coming towards her, pulling back her already short hair into the smallest ponytail anyone had ever seen.

"I don't know why you do that, it's not even on your neck anyway."

Denise grinned. "Makes me feel like I'm a real athlete."

A laugh bubbled up from deep within Meredith and she put her hand over her mouth to cover it up.

"Don't," Denise admonished. "It's good to hear you laugh."

It went without saying between the two of them that Meredith hadn't had much to laugh about for a while.

"It feels good *to* laugh," she admitted.

The moment got a little too heavy and Denise did what she'd gotten best at with the other woman, turned the attention away from her.

"So how far are we going to go today? Are you going to give me a heart attack or just an irregular heartbeat?" she joked.

Meredith knew just how much Denise hated exercise and that said a lot about the person that Denise was. That she came out here everyday, huffing and puffing her way through whatever run Meredith mapped out for them.

"Maybe just an irregular heartbeat. I don't wanna kill ya just yet."

"Thank God for small favors."

With that, the two took off, jogging slowly, but Denise groaned because she knew that soon, they would really start running and that just plain sucked.

"Meredith go for a run?"

It unnerved Liam sometimes how quiet Tyler was when he wanted to be. Sometimes he could come in and out of a room and no one knew it. Even if the room was full of people.

"Yeah, you could just track her you know."

"I know," he said, grabbing his skull coffee cup. "But then I feel like I'm stalking her. It's not a good feeling."

"She still having trouble sleeping?" Liam asked his friend as he had a seat across the table from him.

"Yeah, she thinks I don't know, but I hear her every morning when she wakes up. She's having nightmares, but she won't talk to anybody about them. I keep hoping she'll talk to Denise."

Gently, Liam reminded the other man. "She had a horrible thing happen to her, maybe she doesn't want to talk to anyone about it."

"I want her to talk to me about it. That way I can figure out who the fucker was and then scalp him like my ancestors."

"You know how scary you are saying that as you drink from a skull coffee mug?" Liam deadpanned.

Tyler grinned. "I know. Keeps you on your toes don't it?"

Denise gulped the water from the bottle that Meredith had finally given her. "You love this don't you?" she panted, putting her hand at the stitch on her side.

"Not at all. It's sad that you're having such a hard time with a simple run," Meredith grinned.

"Simple my ass Rager! These are fucking hills. Hills I say!"

"I know, and you're doing a really good job. I really am proud of you."

Denise took a moment to get her breath. "I'm proud of you too."

The moment turned awkward as Meredith turned so that Denise couldn't see her face. "Don't turn away from me. I am proud of you. You've found something that you like doing and you're doing it."

"Only because I know I'm safe here," Meredith argued.

"I worried about you that week after it happened. I didn't think you were ever going to get out of that bed. You've made great strides."

"But I still can't let Tyler sleep in his own bed."

Denise cautiously put her hand on Meredith's arm. "Trust me, when you're ready he'll be ready. No one even looks at your wrong for fear of him."

"I feel like I'm using him," she admitted.

"You're not. You're living your life the only way you know how at this point and truthfully that's all you can ask for. I can't imagine going through what you went through and I'm not saying that out of pity. It's the truth."

But that was the problem wasn't it? All Meredith could feel, when she could actually feel was the pity. The fear. The emptiness. When would it ever change?

24580614R00149

Made in the USA
Charleston, SC
01 December 2013